Richard Peabody is the co-editor of *Mondo Barbie*, *Mondo Elvis*, *Mondo Marilyn*, *Mondo James Dean*, and *Coming to Terms: A Literary Response to Abortion*. His most recent book of poems is *Buoyancy and Other Myths*. His book of stories is *Paraffin Days*. He lives in Washington, DC, where he is co-owner of Atticus Books and Music.

a different

edited by richard peabody

writings by women of the beat generation

beat

Library of Congress Catalog Card Number: 96–725581

A catalogue record for this book is available from the
British Library on request.

The right of the individual contributors to be identified
as the authors of their work has been asserted by them in
accordance with the Copyright, Designs and Patents Act 1988.

See copyright notices pages 232–234

First published in 1997 by Serpent's Tail,
4 Blackstock Mews, London N4, and
180 Varick Street, 10th floor, New York, NY 10014
website: www.serpentstail.com

Cover design by Rex Ray, San Francisco
Set in 10pt Janson and Futura Condensed
by Intype London Ltd
Printed in Finland by Werner Söderström Oy

This book is for Peggy Pfeiffer

A tip of the hat to Kathryn Ugoretz for thinking up the title, and to Carol Bergé for passing it on to me. Big hugs to Janine Vega who I first met in DC in 1978 and who inadvertently gave me the idea. Mucho love to Gretchen Sinclair who gave her all during trying times and the great flood. Plus blessings and heartfelt thanks to Bob and Susan Arnold, Donna Ashley, Eric Baizer, Michael Basinski, David Bianco, Kate Blackwell, John Bowers, Jim Burns, Ann Charters, Carol Christiansen, Dianne Conley, Lucinda Ebersole, Florence B. Eichin, Janice Eidus, David and Vicki Greisman, Derrick Hsu, Jan Kerouac, Brenda Knight, Allan Kornblum, David Kresh, Jay Landesman, M. L. Liebler, Peter London, Betsy J. Loushin, Fred McDarragh, Greg Messina, Richard Miller, Gerald Nicosia, Laurence O'Toole, Simon R. J. Pettifar, Maja Prausnitz, Kevin and Margaret Ring, Bob Sharrard, David Sheridan, Ira Silverberg, Leo Skir, David Stanford, Gunther Stuhlmann, Kenneth Tindall, Laura Ulewicz, Joy Walsh, ruth weiss, Ted Wilentz, and everyone else who helped along the way.

Contents

"Yes, it's all right to blame the men for exploiting the women—or, I think the point is, the men didn't push the women literally or celebrate them. . . . But then, among the group of people we knew at the time, who were the writers of such power as Kerouac or Burroughs? Were there any? I don't think so.

"Were we responsible for the lack of outstanding genius in the women we knew? Did we put them down or repress them? I don't think so. . . .

"Where there was a strong writer who could hold her own, like Diane di Prima, we would certainly work with her and recognize her."

—Allen Ginsberg,
Boulder Sunday Camera Magazine

"I see the girl Joyce Glassman, twenty-two, with her hair hanging down below her shoulders, all in black like Masha in *The Seagull*—black stockings, black skirt, black sweater—but unlike Masha, she's not in mourning for her life. How could she have been, with her seat at the table in the exact center of the universe, that midnight place where so much is converging, the only place in America that's alive? As a female, she's not quite part of this convergence. A fact she ignores, sitting in her excitement as the voices of the men, always the men, passionately rise and fall and their beer glasses collect and the smoke of their cigarettes rises toward the ceiling and the dead culture is surely being wakened. Merely being here, she tells herself, is enough.

"What I refuse to relinquish is her expectancy.

"It's only her silence that I wish finally to give up."

—Joyce Johnson

Introduction

A couple of things you should know. This book is the outgrowth of a class I taught on Beat Writers at Georgetown University in the fall of 1993. There were some fifteen women in that class who'd signed up to learn about Kerouac and company, and might well have benefited more from learning about the women Beats instead. Plus, none of the material by the twenty-six women in this book duplicates any of the material by the seven women this book shares in common with Ann Charters's *Portable Beat Reader* (Viking Penguin, 1992), and duplicates only one poem by one of the three women included in Anne Waldman's *The Beat Book: Poems & Fiction from the Beat Generation* (Shambhala, 1996).

I realize many Beat purists wouldn't make the same choices or selections I have in this anthology. Consider that my editorial prerogative. Margaret Randall and Sandra Hochman appear in Fred W. McDarragh's *Kerouac & Friends: A Beat Generation Album*; Carol Bergé had poems in *Seventh Street: An Anthology from Le Deux Megots*, in *The East Side Scene*, and in *Light Years: The NYC Coffeehouse Poets of the 1960s* anthologies; Mimi Albert and Laura Ulewicz were included in Jim Burns's article "Beat Women" in *Beat Scene #16* from 1993, and that was enough rationale for me.

Arguments could also be made for the inclusion of poets and writers as diverse as Barbara Guest, Rochelle Owens, Grace Paley, Daisy Aldan, Denise Levertov, Jean Garrigue, Patsy Southgate, Gloria Oden, Carolyn Stoloff, Diane Wakoski, Kaye McDonough, and other less-known writers, artists, and coffeehouse scenesters like Hazel Ford, Lenore Jaffee, Elia Kokkinen, Marion Zazeela, Maryanne Raphael, Ruth Fainlight, Rosemary Santini, Mimi Margeaux, Penny Carol, Marcia Lord, Ann Giudici, Mary E. Mayo, Betty E. Taub, Ruth Krauss, Elizabeth Sutherland, Mary Caroline Richards, Anne Wilson, DeeDee Doyle (who published as Sharon Morill), Jan Balas, Jeanne Phillips, Edith Kutash, Fran Sheridan, Sheila Platt, Sally Stern, Madeline Davis, Anne Frost, Anabel Kirby, Alice Pankovits, Francine Marshall, Gloria Tropp, Susan Sherman, Joan Block, L. S. M. Kelly, Susan Gorbea, and Maretta Greer.

I was after a certain feeling. I wanted this collection to be both a rediscovery and a celebration. I wanted a book filled with work that rejoiced in female independence of mind and spirit. Work that would defy conventions and yet speak for women coming of age in both the fifties and sixties, and even beyond. In most cases the material in this anthology is very early work. Many of these women are still writing today, still producing books, but I wanted to focus specifically on the Beat period (roughly 1957–65) and only reprint material that would reflect that period (for the most part) and represent their point of view. I wasn't very interested in works by women writers that focused on the male Beats (save for those cases where it was unavoidable). Instead, I was after a book that put things in perspective and certified some of the early breakthrough work focusing on women's issues that set the cornerstone for what has developed into the Riot Grrrls, angry women, and female outlaws of today. Think of them as the Beat Grrrls. Not much of a stretch. While some may consider this material dated, or not on a par with the work by their Beat male counterparts, remember that this is meant to be something of a historical document, a certification of their existence. Contrary to the established canon—these women were not all invisible or silent, not necessarily hidden in the shadows, some like ruth weiss were always right up there on stage firing their work into the same hip clubs frequented by their better known male counterparts. Whether the men helped or hindered, actively held the women back, ignored female creativity, or consciously treated women as second class citizens is still being debated. The male-defined misogynist social climate of the fifties and sixties gets my vote as the primary culprit. Too many passive women accepted their assigned roles. Others devoted their time and energy to the men, or promoted the men instead of addressing their own work. What better time then to salvage this rich history, to give the women of the arts renaissance called "Beat" a spotlight from which to sound their call to arms, to beat their own drums, the different drums Thoreau wrote about. I don't know about you, but women always seem more in tune to life rhythms than any men I've ever encountered. Their heartbeat rhythm hasn't quit despite unfair neglect. And if *Beat* really means *Beatitude*, who else has been down longer or mistreated more as wife or girlfriend or trophy, and risen up to sing out? Judging from the sarcastic laser of Sheri Martinelli's "Duties of a Lady Female," the more things change, the more they really do stay the same. Her poem is as timely now as it must have been shocking when first published thirty years ago. Proof positive that the women of the Beat generation were carefully observing the men and taking notes. And many still are.

I hope some enterprising publishers see their way to putting a lot of these women back into print, perhaps publishing some of the unpublished manuscripts. So much of this work is scattered in obscure small magazines or chapbooks with minuscule print runs, available only to those who traffic in expensive first editions or venture into library rare book rooms. (Though sadly these scarce items are frequently missing from shelves, stolen, or lost in the system.) Gathering this material in one place then is my bid against obsolescence, unscrupulous book dealers, and petty thievery. Besides, an actual book beats the hell out of Xerox handouts. And, isn't it about time?

—Richard Peabody
Spring 1995/Summer 1996

MIMI ALBERT

from The Second Story Man

I saw him for the second time in Mary's arms. He lay forward, pressed against her, so that his hands and face were hidden from me. Beneath him, Mary too was hidden by the blur of hair which concealed her as she turned from side to side, slowly. And at first I thought she was refusing him, trying to cast him off even as he entered her, that he was an attacker, taking her by force before my eyes.

"What are you doing?" I cried. "What is it?"

Responding to the sound, the man lifted his head blindly, and the sight of his upraised face came to me with the impact of a blow. I knew him. I knew who he was. I had held his image within myself, significant, waiting for recognition. Only it had been above my own head that I had dreamed his features. Above the swell of my own chest that I had willed his out-thrust chin, his lips. I watched him as the breath came from his nose and mouth, and his thin hands moved against her breasts. I knew then that Mary was with him because she wanted him, and not only for herself as she believed, but for the two of us.

For me.

Later I would understand that moment as the end of my time with Mary. Alone with her, I was captured in an interlude of nights and afternoons so filled with her presence that I was granted a reprieve from the usual emotions and fatigues of my own life.

I met her at a party.

"All kinds of people will be there," offered my friend, inviting me.

I was too shy to speak to any of the men. Instead I spoke to Mary.

Mary was drunk. She wore a long coat and a pair of dark rough trousers, like a man's. She leaned against a wall, barely able to stand upright. Her smile was bitchy. Her eyes were the color of cinders. I knew right away that I wanted to be her friend.

I wanted her to teach me what she knew. How to be drunk, and beautiful, and at a party like this without caring, although she wasn't much older than I was, and I was only seventeen.

The smell of pot returns her to me. I came to see her in her empty three room apartment on Avenue C and 12th Street. It was the middle of the summer and she stood naked on the splintered floors and taught me to turn on with a small stone pipe.

"What else do you do?" I wanted to know, when I was high for the first time, and thoroughly baffled. Everyone I knew was going to school.

"I don't do anything else," she said. "This is it."

She didn't like to talk about herself. Gradually, though, she allowed the pieces of her life to fall about me, fragments in a kaleidoscope. With a word she dismissed her family.

"My father is a surgeon. Very handy with a scalpel."

School had been an expensive university upstate. Escape was first a dozen men—most of the football team, the chemistry professor, the gropers after dances—then one abortion, performed in an empty apartment in New York.

"After which," she asked me, her grey eyes gleaming with bitterness, "why should I go back?"

Her first year in the city was spent in a state of loneliness so intense that it had the quality of a novitiate. It had made her whole and totally hard, like metamorphosed stone.

She said she needed no one. Still, both of us must have known it was a lie.

Certainly she didn't need me. I thought that she had more planned for me that day, but one of her lovers came and they took a bath together while I sat there, and she made me read to them from a book of Salinger's short stories. "To Esmé, With Love and Squalor." Later she accepted me because I confirmed her existence. I ran alongside her in the streets, I sat with her in bars and coffeeshops. I lent her clothing, gave her money, bought her food. In return she presided over my first sexual adventures with the amused aloofness of a priestess inaugurating secret rites.

"You go with him," she'd say to me, selecting some man who she thought was suitable. Then she might stand and listen at the door. I did everything she told me to do. But she never offered me any tenderness. Her distance was the result of her own honesty. Why should she have mercy for others, or for herself? She believed compassion was only another form of weakness.

Now I remember our brief season together only as a series of escapades. I vacated my childhood without amnesty or treaty; I too was an escapee. One night I fled my father's house. I came to Mary's apartment because I had nowhere else to go.

"Let me stay," I begged. She said nothing. Still, she didn't throw me out.

I starved with her without complaint, fearful that anything might make her change her mind. Neither of us had jobs or money.

At last she said, "I know what to do," and putting on heavy raincoats, we descended to the local supermarket.

"Follow me," she said, and taught me how to skulk between the aisles ramming cans of food into my pockets without getting caught. I was proud of my own daring, but Mary insisted on stealing only elaborate, unsatisfying foods. She stuffed small overpriced jars of caviar, smoked oysters and liver pâté into her coat, unable to refrain from laughter, maybe hoping to be caught merely for the adventure. The clerks watched us with suspicion, waiting for evidence.

"Why caviar?" I would ask her. "Why snails? I hate eccentric food. Why don't we swipe a tenderloin once in a while?"

The checkers, plain sour women wearing green smocks and hairnets, turned their heads and lifted their eyebrows like alerted animals as we cantered down the aisles, our pockets clanking with bottles and jars. Returning to her apartment the two of us would fall down on the kitchen floor and laugh, already nauseated by the opened cans of smoked oysters, the short round jars of lumpfish caviar, the olives in salty water.

Sometimes too, becoming slowly high and having no one else to talk to, she might tell me stories about herself and listen as well to mine. I would feel then that I did know her after all, better than anyone else. That she and I were friends.

But I always knew that time was going to carry us away from one another. Running up the stairs that last night, feeling chilled and tense because the first winter stillness had fallen upon the city, I thought suddenly and without cause,

Maybe this will be the last time. The end of things. She'll be standing at the top of the stairs and she'll tell me, "Go away. I don't want you any more." Or else she won't be there at all. The apartment will be empty, ransacked. Everything gone.

I climbed.

Or *maybe*, I thought, *she could be there with someone new. A man she wants to live with. And she'd ask me to get out.*

Gradually it occurred to me that my discomfort centered about the man whose name I knew but didn't want to remember. To pronounce it would be to reveal a secret, although I didn't know whose secret it was nor why it should be so carefully guarded. Until I tried the door and found it unlocked, and flung it open on the room.

Later I would remember that as a moment I had always expected. For nights, before her door, I must have anticipated it, so the shock should at least have been softened for me. But when I realized who the man was, upon her, my impulse was to slam the door and turn back into the hall. I stood for a moment with my eyes closed. Then Mary called me firmly, like a hostess at a party scolding a backward guest.

"Oh, Anna!" she cried. "Come in!"

In obedience to this I opened the door again. I came slowly now, with caution. She smiled at me from the center of the bed. Her hair was spread out around her. The light was on, directly over them. It glared on their skin.

Her eyes were open. Her expression was innocent, even angelic. By insisting that all actions were simple, on the surface, she denied the existence of shame. This, like all the moments of her life, was illuminated by her honesty. She had never hung curtains in her rooms, but stood naked in the morning light, her skin as white and hard as some rare stone. She dressed without haste before the open windows, daring the world to find fault with her. This candor was her charm. It was the magic with which she manipulated life. She glanced at me now from the center of the bed, her arms and legs twined about him, and her eyes, watching me, were both contemptuous and warm.

"Come and sit down," she said. Her face was flushed and merry. She almost laughed. I believe that had she been able she would have cleared a place for me beside them.

I sat down on a chair near the bed. I was astonished at my ability to sit so easily, to light a cigarette. I tried to move my eyes away from them but found it impossible. I was already beyond my depth. I was forced to return to them again and again.

The man ignored me. Perhaps he was too busy to notice, or maybe he didn't really care. He moved above her with the same awkward intensity with which I had seen him walk. Her face turned soft and unconscious of itself and she looked away from me. His profile was turned to me but I caught the expression of his mouth, his lips twisted and distorted with what looked like pain. And beneath his body and my eyes, Mary moved naturally and calmly, letting her mouth fall open so that spit coiled slowly between her lips. Her eyes rolled back. I knew that she was pleased by our mutual homage, by the attention of his body and my gaze upon her. Together as they rose and fell they were perfectly matched; the form and motion of their figures corresponded in rhythm and strength. He reared and thrashed, his hands fluttered down along her sides. Suddenly he sobbed as if he had been wounded. I wanted to leap up from my chair and run away, but I couldn't. I stayed where I was and waited. He screamed. I didn't understand. At first I thought that it was merely satisfaction; later I was just as convinced that it was merely rage. Mary lay too still. Her head was turned away. Her skin was pale. Her mouth was open. I knew then that he had a power over her which no one had ever had before. She was afraid.

He had gone beyond our reach. He sighed, falling backwards, letting her go, "I'm finished. Dead."

Then they were quiet. Their hair was pasted to the skin with sweat. They lay with their eyes open and their hands across their chests, like corpses. The sight of their bodies joined together in that room, beneath that yellow light, has long since become part of the debris which fills my dreams. I gave myself to the spectacle of their love. I opened to it as we open to those moments which most deeply move us. I believe that even my own acts have never affected me more powerfully than this.

She looked up from the center of the bed.

"A cigarette," she said, extending her arm.

She took one from my hand, pretending not to notice that my fingers shook. We shared it slowly, dragging on it in turn, the three of us. They came out of her sheets as from combat. He smiled. Satisfaction left him vulnerable, childlike. His mouth was very soft. He pressed his lips together, taking the cigarette from her and drawing on it.

"All right," he said, looking at me. "What's this?"

His voice revealed his origins, just as the bowed roll of his walk revealed his time on the sea.

"What's this?" he said again, and smoked. Calmly, like a man in a waiting room. Exposed completely, he didn't trouble to pull up the sheets. He was both daring us and showing his contempt for us. His shoulders rose above arms in which the veins were blue and twisted, forming knots of tint beneath the skin.

"Anna's a friend," Mary said. "She's been staying with me."

"Two women are never friends," he pronounced. He said it all in a rush, with his arms stretched back above his head. His entire body was hairless except for the auburn curls at his underarms and groin. He surveyed me casually yet with care, as if just asked to service both of us.

Mary sat up naked, and the sight of her breasts exposed to me angered him.

"Put something on," he dictated.

But she said, "It doesn't matter," and climbed out of bed. "Anna doesn't care. We live together."

He went red. I expected him to hit her. He scowled and turned his face to the wall. Shaking, I stood. My chair fell backwards.

"I'm going." I trembled as I spoke. I understood then exactly how I was being used. Mary went to my side, taking one of my arms between her hands, and held me there. Her head was very close to mine. There was strength in her hands.

"I'm getting out," I said again.

He and I sat on opposite sides of the bed, looking at one another. He didn't remember that he had met me once before. Mary held me. Suddenly he swivelled sharply and extended a single, grimy hand, almost as he would to another man.

"Florian Rando," he informed me. I took his hand. The clasp was swift and cold. "How are you?" he said, automatically. He bothered now to look down at himself, outstretched on the sheets, and to pull a blanket over his naked hips. Mary let me go and walked away. To my amazement when she came back into the room, she was fully dressed.

"I didn't do it for you," she teased, kicking him gently. "I was cold."

"Don't let you get away with anything, does she?" He watched her with affection. "Got a sharp tongue, too."

Already then he was protective of her, and he was proud. *So it's gone that far*, I thought. I forced a smile, taking out my last pack of cigarettes. It was all I had.

"Help yourselves," I offered, and they did. I sat between them, numbed by what I felt. I wanted to give them everything. Even to strip myself naked, if it meant pleasing them.

"So you're a friend of Mary's, are you?" he said at last, breathing out the smoke. His eyes travelled over my face, and I wondered what he saw there. Some sign, some mark of the condition which he no doubt suspected? I could imagine him saying to Mary, "Why you got some kid living with you? She a dyke?" as though that arrangement, only that, would appear logical to him.

"Yes," I said. By comparison to Mary I knew I was ugly and weak. For some reason this even eased my pain. If he didn't want me, it might be easier for him to share himself with me. (This is the consolation always offered to the plain woman; that, beneath desire, she's less dangerous, can be confided in.) But I realized this only later. Then he was strangely compassionate, and his kindness was the ultimate insult. Still, if he was going to treat me like another man, I decided to behave like one. I made my movements clumsy and strong. I took a bill from my pocket, and threw it across the bed to Mary.

"Here," I said. My voice was harsh and strange. I threw the money desperately. It was my last. I knew that in throwing it away I too was free, if only for an instant.

"Go down and get us something to eat," I said.

"And some liquid refreshment too," he added, admiring the size of the bill. He leaned across the bed and picked it up, handing it to Mary before he turned back to me. His eyes were frank and clear, his face indicated gratitude and friendship.

"Nothing like a drink to clear the air." And to my astonishment there was something almost sheepish in his smile.

We sat around the table together like three old friends, sharing sandwiches and mixing rye with water. They laughed and talked. Maybe they were thinking that they might never see one another again. They still believed that they didn't need one another, that they meant nothing to each other. If she noticed any difference in her reaction to him, she blamed it on his skill in bed.

"You're very good," she told him.

"So are you," he said.

Neither of them noticed the similarity or the emptiness of their speech, or knew that they were being duped.

For the first time that night I heard his laughter, delivered between compressed lips. As he drank his voice got almost shrill. From time to time he interrupted his own flow of words and turned to her with a fierce direct request, demanding and wheedling at the same time.

"Mary! Are you listening?"

"Yes," she always said.

I sat between them, unable to speak. I had become their witness against my will. I looked into his face in the glare of the light, and I accepted it all.

"She will do," I thought, "what I could not."

And it seemed natural that she should end with him and I should be alone, and watching them.

Later, drunk and heavy with the whiskey, I leaned against his shoulder and muttered, "Crazy about you, man. She always was. She always will be. Made for each other, you two."

He placed his arm about my shoulders gently, and I felt that they exchanged looks and smiled above me at the table. In the morning, waking alone in the little room she let me have, I was going to remember and cry out in rage. Now in the kitchen, drunk, I loved them both. What could I do but witness and note the events of their life together? I knew that they loved one another before they did; I felt their passion grow as if it was my own. But I knew too that had it been my own it couldn't have caused me such intense and solemn joy. For I am rooted to earth by hesitation and by the caution which keeps me safe, and even by the very words which bind me here.

CAROL BERGÉ

tessa's song

i.

sleep	sleep
the shy girl	the pretty one
woodwandering	slipping by trees
from the loves	faster he runs
warm after her	she runs

sleep	sleep
the doe eye	the wild girl
knows	goes shrilling
shies a shoulder	after
touched too fast	a long chase

ii.

i talk filth and energy
pissing at them the vacant horror
of my lofts and days
passed from my pennsylvania mother
like dung or philosophy
my brother is cerberus for me
but i miss those fields
o i miss those fields and the
barns hexed sideways for witches

iii.

from my slackjaw eyes
the fifth boybaby will fall soon
they come at me and fill me with child
and i cannot stop this
it speaks of love   five fathers
old sweater on my fat wondering belly
and my white skinny arms full of holes

iv.

it is beautiful where i go
green leaves falling into brown-water pool
no sound   no sound at all
so gentle   there are no voices

when the leaves fall into water
no sound   just the sight of ripples
if i sit and do not move a while
i am there again
my open eyes see the water
see the falling leaves   the water

once it was hills and meadows
now i go to this other place
with leaves and brown water   peaceful
no one can come to me there
it is like death   and lovely

peaceful   lovely where i go

v.

give me something   some slacks
or i will rummage salvation army again
i move there through underclothes
in my point-faced afternoon
to find a way of facing things
that might fit me
these days   shuffling along 8th street
in my sort of bedroom slippers
all cold except my loose bellyfolds
my world is flat
i move from it in any leaving way
since i gave them my fifth boy
i forget pennsylvania   my mother's face
which man goes into me and when it was
and all the faces of my face

vi.

make me a magic
what does one wear for dying

my brother
what kind of shirt connotes a giving up
which color to show years
for a child hurt into now
into dreamless violent streets
stitch me a painted shirt
with gold needles
and my face as it has looked each year
along the borders

vii.

lovely to grow a child up
till her braids are long
till she wears skirts again
lovely to grow a child up
the calm peaceful days
the peaceful nights into now
the feeding and the loving
lovely to watch a child grow

viii.

shit i hate those hospitals
dont you   quit grabbing my pills
you make me whine that way
gimme gimme gimme gimme it was
better the last time move over
eyes and you are kind to me
i do not recognize you but
i am sweating and tweaking with
your kindness   move over   gimme

ix.

is this the turbulence of which
you spoke then pilot
about which you joke now
minutes before we crash

1960

Pavane for the White Queen
The Loved Wife Falling Slowly Awake
for JBK

I. *In the Rooms of Music*

Not as the word death. But
as confusion: memory of bells
into voices of broken bells,
sound of torn strings: songs
into this silent scream. Not
the keening of the loveless,
the ugly in their disarrayed
skins. Who have not tasted
rooms of music shaped as eyes
through flesh: woman near man.
Not as the word death. But
as samisen gone suddenly mute,
shut memory of night voices
into sharp shriek: crackling,
as when eyes shatter. I move
toward your empty room. Begin
stopping the usual gestures.
To cease listening. The sound
of music in eye-shaped rooms
having stopped with one note.

II. *In the Street of Eyes*

Eventually, it happens. I move
into our streets, slowly. I see
his head; its shape is almost yours.
He is not you. At first I thought.
Or that man. Or that. A tall man,
near the door. In that car. The
park yesterday. Shops. It is a
slow nightmare of wrong faces, turn
of cheek, memory of your jaw line,
eyes, the way your feet would
strike the pavement and pivot you.
Shadows of occasional hell, as
someone unconsciously imitates you.

I am supposed to know where you are,
that no city contains you whole.
Yet this odd stumbling over raw or
stunning hints: this looking into
the sudden stranger's unloved face!

III. In the Dust House

This furniture that was ours
talks clumsily about our loving.
I thought we were bound by wood,
leather, cloth of our own skins:
now my thinner dark skull stops
before reaching our silk pillows.
How to move, to sleep, now that
your warm skull has become stone!
where marble dust congeals to
walls, rooms down which my feet
run noiselessly and motionless
in thick night or sharp dreams
cushioning one shrill red day:
God! that your feet are gone!
and mine, marking out the hours,
perform a mockery of minuets
amid the velvet and the marble.
Candles, sunlight that glinted
when your eyes shaped our days
turn now to flares of anguish,
all flames go dull, the magic
slips through my fingers, marks
blood on parquet, on old satin,
the mourners note my vertebrae
impressed into my white cape.
It was this castle we once lit,
our lives parallel to love, to
deep sleep, gentle confidences.
With the same cry as that child
who bears your eyes, I am turned
toward the watchers, in their
terrible distance of armchairs,
of pages: my cheeks and ribs

blanched, immolated beneath a
careful avalanche of pale powder
and papers: and am remembering
our hands, our feet, as it was
when we moved unaware in rooms
of careless laughter, banquets,
beds warm into a sleep of love
where you have gone without me.
The sounds, the rooms fragment
and drift, it is too quiet, the
love having stopped with you,
the castle flakes like paint,
I become my own skin and turn
before their eyes into marble,
lit from within by your face,
voice stilled by one red note.

1963–1964

Chant for Half the World

The women as richesse of liquid chocolate
between their legs beneath their navels
The women like their own shrieks
glass curse of their angular legs
"in the way the women move" in agony in
graceless flounderings on the smooth
dance floor of their lonely manipulations

The women in their floured eyes
their skin mansions such gifts slipped
over inner eyes till fur finally grows
into the fake charity of the yoni

First girlchild becomes servile
Second loses its birthright escutcheon
Third girl has no face fourth is shadow
first girlchild leads schools
second becomes maker of delicate symbols
third creates old specific buttons
fourth is the voiceless farmer's wife

Women with their liberal blackened teeth
moving on round beds above oracles
under stone men as *idolos* of themselves
High priestesses of unnameable objects
called miscarriages or beetroots

Teeth gapped to equal each child lost
Each lost child never bridged
The women breast to breast across empty
across lava-strewn bitter plains
facing lidless eyes of the majestic surgeons
who demand they empty their wombs
of the quintuplet dolls shaped like "husband"
Women offering full teats to
men with infant faces who drink with mouths
the violet of sleep or of healed circumcision

The women their flowing words of casuistry
tennisballs stuffed into mouths
ping pong balls into eye sockets

volleyball up anus marbles in earcurves
nostrils filled with buckshot
Words falling like terrible stars from the yoni

What does she say how gesture like silk
how shed skin in the burn of his piercing
how bend how move between rooms like shoji
Sound of brrrrütsss brrrrütsss smooth
as skin under birch branches of the sauna
"to make the skin glow"
or Lord Sir King Masoch robed advancing
toward la marquesa Mademoiselle de Sade
exchanging vows and blows

The women near men in thick dance forgetting
honey in joints in hollow of bones
of cunt eyes furred away from how it was
with limbs not wooden but la belle sauvage
The forgetting forgotten
across inflamed glass dancefloors
Laughter a bite of betel teethmarks
hair into oiled peaks as foretold
away from false minuets away
from degradation of boot lingam
shined and polished beyond identification

Man reach for me i am firm open i am
waiting in the dark place which has
all secrets i have
have lust as deep as you can reach
But take off that skin that hair shirt
choose between forks of tongue
or is it a forked prick you speak to me with

The women as kosmotics
wombs tipped crazily toward the source light
careening toward the meteorite of fuck
Words of the recent typical insane poet
gone into seed and fat lyrics
behaving like a giant bearded night moth
which refutes its genes assaying day
Saying moon is man sun is woman

Ah better to be content as bucolic barley
than to outguess the sex of planets

Tragedies of women their toothlessness
having had the wombs wormed like sick kits
having little to do but notice how hills
recall flesh as it might have been
having been bound from infancy to boards
which at other times held their own roast flesh
ready for the obsidian knives
The accurate synaptic traceries prohibited
turned instead into lightning on film
overexposed and comically brilliant
Position of woman in relation to a tree

If you do it against a tree and it is with love
it is as valid as between silk coverlets
he once told his classroom of Vassarites
and was fired for illuminating fifty gates
Or Agnes de Mille leaping in a dark church
given over now to bowings and deep genuflections
antithesis of the good fuck or dance
All the women gone into black for a pope
trained to despise half of humanity

The women walking with eyes turned inward
their fine navels cabbages of joy
along streets paved with vegetables
The women moving seeded and buttered
offering packaged suicides to young men
harnesses cut from the Fallopian tubes
tied with the deaths of their fathers

The rich women of animalskins
waists slanted in memory of wellsprings
stained with sun with come with breastmilk
The women coppered and grafted into love
reaching smiling toward the lingam
The women with blood with liquid chocolate
shrieking letting loose hand and hair
The women walking as memory of man

Winter 1965

Etching

(in memory: Walter Benedict)

One friend last year
had too many bad trips
trying to find himself
Found himself instead
in Bellevue and lost
Sad sad sad now I have
only a self-portrait
a proof on newsprint
he once gave to me

Today Halma comes by
saying she has something
to leave with me before
she splits for the coast
I am afraid it will be
a full-size paper effigy
of you as I knew you

Ah how acid has eaten
the flesh of my friends
leaving a papery rustle

1967

CAROLYN CASSADY

from Off the Road: My Years with Cassady, Kerouac, and Ginsberg

Soon after the beginning of 1950 I answered the phone to hear a low, brash Eastern voice say cheerily, "Hi! Carolyn? This is Diana Hansen in New York. I suppose Neal's told you he lives with me here? How are you? How is Cathy?"

I pulled the telephone to the couch and sat down; my heart had either stopped or was lodged somewhere where it didn't belong. "No" was all I could utter but she surged ahead, just as though we were old friends.

"Well, as you know by now, I'm sure, you and Neal were never right for each other, and since you've kicked him out never to darken your door again, ha, ha—you're absolutely right, of course—and I know how glad you are to be free. So, you see, we want to ask a favor of you— that is, Neal asked me to ask if you'll divorce him. It seems I'm pregnant, and I know *you'll* understand that we want to get married as soon as possible—give the little brat a name and all that, you know—ha, ha."

A cold mass now replaced my solar plexus, and disbelief chanted "No, no, no, no" through my head. I'd never even thought of this possibility, never. No one else could have his babies. How could it be? All my strength was needed to push sound into words.

"Why doesn't Neal ask me himself?"

"Oh, no reason. He just asked me to. I was going to call you, anyway. You and I have a lot to talk about. I've been dying to call you for just ages. I hope I have a girl. If I do, I'll name her Jennifer. What do you think? Isn't that a darling name? You know, we have this great apartment, Carolyn. You'd love it. I've decorated it all up like the Village with travel posters, you know? Neal's writing his book, and he's been so good at staying at it. I'm afraid I spoil him terribly. I just wait on him hand and foot . . . and he never goes out, just likes staying here at home with me. His friends come over a lot, though. I have to admit I don't care much for his friends—awfully lowbrow, you know what I mean—except Jack. I like Jack, and then Allen, of course—that's how we met, through Allen, at a party. But the other people that hang around aren't good for Neal. They sponge, and we've barely enough money for ourselves. I work—I'm a model—I love to work . . ." And on and on and on. Through it all, the only words that stuck in my brain were "I'm pregnant." Please, God, make it not true.

"Well, whaddya say, Carolyn? You'll get the divorce? We'll pay for it, but how long do you think it will take?"

"I'll only do it if Neal asks me himself. Goodbye."

This was the bitterest pill I have ever had to swallow, and it never completely dissolved. In a day or two I received a typewritten letter, signed by Neal but obviously dictated by Diana. It hurt and disgusted me that he would allow her to do this, but I supposed it was in his nature to try to give everyone what they wanted of him.

In martyred agony I hired a lawyer, but we had a problem finding grounds for a divorce. Not that there weren't plenty, rather there were too many whose nature we didn't care to air in public. The Hinkles had returned by now and Helen agreed to serve as my witness and the legal wheels were set in motion.

On Thursday, 26 January, I was alone in the office while the doctor was on her rounds, when I knew my time had come. I still felt fine, so I completed all the unfinished business in the office, then took the cable car home. I had a cup of coffee with Helen, packed my bag and called a cab.

The hospital was overflowing, so I was parked on a guerney in the hall and given a caudal anesthetic. But Jami hardly gave me time to enjoy it, for an hour and a half later she arrived, entering the world in a storeroom. She lay screaming on a counter until a nurse remembered to take her away. Her damp hair stood out from her head in long black spikes, and with her eyes swollen from the drops, she had a distinctly oriental look. Consequently, when later in the afternoon a strange man entered my room and sympathized at length for my having had a Mongoloid baby, I had no reason to doubt him and merely sighed, "What next?" When I asked my doctor what to do about it, he went into mild shock and exposed the error: wrong room, wrong Mrs. Cassady.

This time I was home in three days, and Helen left the next. I was to consider this time off from work as my two-week vacation. It was two weeks but no vacation, Cathy being only seventeen months old. The new sitter had to be paid exactly the sum I earned, but my employer proved herself an angel by installing an extension of her office phone in my house so that I could work part-time from home and split my pay with the sitter.

The divorce suit was filed exactly a month after Jami's birth. Diana wrote me every day from the time she had first called, letters written on yellow lined paper in a large childish hand. At least twice a week she'd telephone, spending $25.00 to tell me how broke she was. So nearly every other afternoon I'd type letters in reply, generally contradicting her opinions about Neal, arguing furiously at her arbitrary pronouncements and illogical conclusions about me.

But throughout, my real motive was to keep in touch with Neal, and much of what I wrote was aimed at winning his approval and convincing him of my remorse at having sent him away. At the time, however, I wasn't fully conscious of this motive, and as I was constantly bombarded with the fact of Diana's pregnancy, I tried to believe that all was really over, forever.

In spite of Diana's impatience, my day in court didn't arrive until late in June. The large courtroom, musty and varnished, overwhelmed me—I'd only seen them in the movies, and I was nervous and miserable. We drew a woman judge who was renowned in San Francisco, and I felt all the more intimidated.

My lawyer was quite timid herself, and barely spoke above a whisper. Even though her prepared list of complaints against Neal had been watered down so that I hardly recognized him, the judge became furious. Gasping, she burst out with "Wait, wait—I'm going to postpone this hearing until we can find that young man! I want to have a talk with him. How can he be so irresponsible? Two small children!"

From the witness stand I flung a horror-stricken look at my lawyer, shaking my head. She got up and said, "Please, Your Honor, we'd prefer to settle it now."

The judge turned to Neal's lawyer and asked, "Where is Mr. Cassady?"

He stood up and said, "He's in Mexico getting married."

I stared at my lawyer, she stared at me, Helen's mouth dropped open, and the courtroom was silent. The judge recovered first, groaned, banged her gavel and said, "Interlocutory degree granted." I was granted $100 a month child support and $1 for alimony; the legal reasoning behind the latter escapes me.

And so it was over. All but the year to wait for the divorce to become final. Here was another painful blow I'd dealt my family: their first divorce. After their reaction to my premarital pregnancy, I had been evasive about my married life, but I would be unable to keep this from them, even if I wanted to.

Diana was now nearly five months along. I hadn't forgotten what it felt like, and I tried to do unto her as I would be done to. After all, I too had been careless, knowing Neal was already married. But I did feel bitter towards Diana, which I thought was justified because she had known Neal had other children to care for. Only later could I face the probability that he had been as persuasive with her as he had with me, convincing her that she was the "only," the "right" woman for him.

Since California law required a year's wait, I couldn't see that my divorce was of much help, and neither obviously did Diana and Neal. He had gone to Mexico to obtain a quickie. I wondered where the money was coming from for all these divorces, especially when I had to hear daily accounts of their dire lack of funds. I suspected Neal had seen an opportunity to obtain a sizeable store of marijuana, and my guess was corroborated by a letter he wrote Jack later, describing his trip and his search for their old "connection," saying he "picked up Elich's Gardens [one of their code names for tea] in New Victoria."

When Neal's railroad call-back telegram arrived, he hastened back to New York, and I was allowed a blessed few days' respite from Diana's communiqués. Even with no papers to prove it, he convinced her he had obtained the divorce, and they were bigamously married in New Jersey on 10 July. Two hours later Neal took the train to "St. Louis and the west; Carolyn and the babies my impending hope," he wrote to Jack.

Immediately he left her, Diana was on to me again, writing me her version of the wedding and saying "I am ashamed of myself for my 'worries' while Neal was away. I shouldn't be such a baby." She explained that Neal hadn't been able to find a job in New York to cover the "Mexican business," saying that was the only reason why he had returned to the railroad, and gave me another penny-by-penny account of her financial status—" . . . none of your concern as long as you get your $101."

As logic is one of my standbys, and as I had a fixed desire to maintain some privacy about my own husband and affairs, every word in her letters seemed to me uncannily devised to drive me mad. "I expect Neal will visit you and the kids this weekend," she wrote. "I don't know what arrangements you'll want to make about his seeing Cathy and Jami. But please be nice to him—he does love them and they *are* his children, too . . . I also think *you*'ll find him a good person . . . See you all in a month or so, I hope . . ." To see her was the very last thing I wanted. It appeared as though bludgeoning was the only way to get through to her, and I was positive I wouldn't be able to control my exasperation if I met her in the flesh.

Neal arrived on my doorstep on the afternoon of 14 July. There's no use denying that my heart leaped at the sight of him, but I did my best not to show it, and backed away from his proffered embrace . . . the embrace I'd been yearning for for almost a whole year.

I attempted some off-hand small talk, but Neal ignored it and walked slowly and softly around the house, gazing reverently at everything, like a man returned from the dead. Barely audibly he said, "Oh, darling . . . you don't know how great it is to be *home*."

"Unh, hunh, I'm sure, Neal, but you can cool all that. It's a bit late for such sentiments. You are entitled to see your children, of course, if you want to. You won't recognize Cathy, and of course, you've never seen Jami." I ground a mental heel on a rising urge to share their growing up with him. "Help yourself to coffee, if you'd like. I'll get them up from their naps."

Neal took no notice of my reactions, persevering in his own game. And, as this history too often relates, he won me over again. He continued his silent reverence, holding and rocking Jami, while looking his special look beyond her to me. Speaking softly to Cathy and stroking her hair, he continued to try and hold my eyes with his soulful gaze. I moved about cleaning up, but he rose and blocked my path or followed me if I dodged him, building the tension between us. It was a game we both knew well.

He finally got around to the inevitable request to move back in with us, but I was firm. "Certainly not—not a chance. After all, you were the one who wanted the divorce, not me. You've swapped us for another family now, so let's quit while we're ahead. You've really gone too far this time, Neal. I've had enough, and I've a good start on my own independence. I certainly don't want to 'start all over again, shudder shudder' as you said in your farewell note."

I tried to put some conviction into my words. Oh, I knew it was the best thing to do, all right, but why would my feelings never correspond?

I didn't let him move in, but he was there most of the time when not at work, insisting he had "the right to get his hundred dollars' worth," as Diana had said. I had been so lonely after Helen left, and he made me feel pretty and desirable again; he was wooing once more, and all the old charm, devotion, helpfulness, kindness, and consideration I'd loved him for in the beginning, was poured in my direction. I thoroughly enjoyed being sought after, but by this time I'd had enough practice to affect indifference and prolong the return of my confidence and security. I insisted on our divorced status being maintained, partly to punish Neal and partly to protect myself from my own desires, and I hoped thus to strengthen my determination to remain free.

ELISE COWEN

At the acting class
The perfect paper daffodil
Upstages us all

....

Dear God of the bent trees of Fifth Avenue
Only pour my wilful dust up your veins
And I'll pound your belly-flat world
In praise of small agonies
Suck sea monsters off Tierra del Fuego
Fuck your only begotten cobalt dream
To filter golden pleasure through your apple glutted heaven
Filter the uncircumcized sin of my heart.

Death I'm coming
Wait for me
I know you'll be
at the subway station
loaded with galoshes, raincoat, umbrella, babushka
And your single simple answer
to every meaning
Incorruptible institution
Listen to what she said
"There's a passage through the white cabbages"
High and laughing through 3 hours

                        Faithful paranoid
                        It's all One to you
                                    isn't it
                        real, that is,
                        Literal
                        enough
To find a snoozing place among thick visions
                till she'll stumble
                over you
Or wait till rot down
                with the
                majesty orange
                she stuck on
                        her finger

Real as the worn green
hideabed I brood on
Never hearing clearly enough
to remember

Or openarmed at the passage end

The homeless
Who lights in her/from her/is
(Her moving human perfection)
Waits for no one
Not even you

I took the skin of corpses
And dyed them blue for dreams
Oh I can wear these *everywhere*
(I sat *home* in my jeans).

I cut the hair of corpses
And wove myself a wreath
Finer than silk or wool I thought
And shivered underneath

I cut the ears of corpses
To make myself a hood—
Warmer than forget-me-nots
I paid for that in blood.

I robbed the eyes of corpses
So I could face the sun
But all the days had cloudy skies
And I had lost my own.

From the sex of corpses
I sewed a union suit
Esther, Solomon, God himself
Were humbler than my cock.

I took the thoughts of corpses
To buy my daily needs
But all the good in all the stores
Were neatly labled Me.

I borrowed heads of corpses
To do my reading by
I found my name on every page
And every word a lie.

Now when I meet the spirits
In who's tappings I am jailed
They buy me wine or read a book
No one can make my bail

When I become a spirit
(I'll have to wait for life)
I'll sell *my* deadly body
To the student doctor's knife.

I wanted a cunt of golden pleasure
                  purer than heroin
To honor you in
A heart big enough to take off
                  your shoes and stretch out
To honor you in
                  Double bed heart like a
                  meadow in Yosemite
To take your ease in
                  Imagination clear & active as
                        sunny tidepools.
To serve up good talk with dinner
                  Soul like your face before you
                        were born
To glory you in
                  breast, hair, fingers,
                  whole city of body
In your arms all night

If it weren't for love I'd snooze all day
Stretched on the mat
Window at my feet
Colored scrap wool childhood afghan
Up to my chin
Music & news
And stories of
Whalers
Oh warm and lovely
But something shoves me
Half dressed
Down the stairs to the telephone
He Ho Nobody home
Imagination!
You'd make me run up & down
the Statue of Liberty steps
All
    Day
        Long
Till I learned to fly.

....

The sound now in the street is the echo of a long
        horn ringing in my ears
My belly gurgles at the knife line
Embracing
Meat, meat
To fuck, to eat
Grind the sleeping homes between my teeth
Love turned bread
Crumbs in the bed

"Trust yourself—but not too far
El Paso fortune on the weighing machine
Sunday trolley/
          full of fleshly Mexicans going to
Mexico (Juarez) just over the
border—not me
"Gone to Mexico—gone home"
          Gone to
                Death
"Death"

          Joke—someone drops pointed paper
          cups (one by one—into the
          long plastic container—
          next to the watercooler
          in the office) and they are falling—
          slowly—and make no
          sound in my ears

LEO SKIR

Elise Cowen: *A brief memoir of the fifties*

I was working in the Welfare office.

> *Someone called me to the phone. I can't remember who.*
> *"Hello. Leo?" the voice on the telephone said.*
> *"Yes," I said. "What is it, Carol?"*
> *"Have you heard about Elise?" she said.*
> *"You mean that she's not going to Florida?"*
> *"No," said Carol, "she jumped out the window. From her parents' apartment. The seventh story."*
> *"Is she dead?" I said.*
> *"She was killed instantly," said Carol.*
> *There was more talk. Then the conversation ended. I hung up and tried to go back to work. . . .*

Elise was dead.

Allen was in Bombay.

I wrote him that night, getting a reply about a week later: He wrote:

> I hope everybody is not scared or plunged further into painful dreams by Elise's hints. None of the dream systems is real, not even deaths. The self that sees all the plots is worth attention, not the plots. That's as far as I know. Good luck—ALLEN

I had met her in 1949 at Hechalutz Hatzair's Zionist training farm in Poughkeepsie. It was Thanksgiving and already very cold in upstate New York. I was seventeen and a Columbia Freshman. Being seventeen was pretty old in our Youth Movement whose members usually went to Israel not to college. I was Movement leader. I had hung behind in America out of fear and asthma.

I was asthmatic that day, wheezing in the cold downstairs room at the farmhouse. The cold was seeping in through the windows. Almost everyone but me was out picking corn or throwing fertilizer on the earth.

I looked out the window at the workers. I was eating a piece of bread spread with colorless margarine.

Then she was there. Elise. Looking like so many of our Jewish girls, the sallow complexion, black lusterless hair bound with a rubber band, a diffident sulky air.

I introduced myself. She was not a Movement member.

"Why not?" I asked.

"I don't want to go to Israel," she said.

"Is there a place for you in America?" I said.

"No," she said.

"Is there some other country you are planning to go to?"

She smiled, embarrassed, the smile half-dissolving behind the thick lenses of her glasses. She pushed her finger nervously against the bridge of the glasses.

"Not yet," she said.

I didn't see her again at any Movement meetings or when I came back to the city.

I didn't see her again until my Senior year at college. I was a member of the Players and we were producing *Henry IV: Part I*. I was Peto. I had only one good line. "*No, no. They were not bound.*"

There was a girl who assisted in the dressing room. She told me she knew someone who knew me.

"Who?" I said.

"Elise Cowen," she said.

"I don't remember her," I said.

"She's a friend of a friend of yours," she said.

"I have no friends," I said. "There are no friends." (A quote from Aristotle.)

Later that evening I visited my friend Pittsburgh John, a rich gentile son of a Pittsburgh manufacturer. Frank was in deep analysis.

He was not at home, but a girl was there.

It was Elise.

She was very nice, very shy, soft-spoken. She didn't ask me why I wasn't in Israel, or if I would be going. I was no longer a Zionist. I was a neurotic Columbia student. So was Pittsburgh John. So was Elise. Being neurotic together.

She had brought over her Woodie Guthrie records, 78 shellacs. She had brought them from her parents' home in Washington Heights, to her little furnished room across the street from Pittsburgh John's. Her room had no phonograph but Pittsburgh John's did.

Pittsburgh John and Elise and I had many pleasant evenings

together. When I was with Pittsburgh John he would talk about his *relationship* with Elise, and Elise would talk about her *relationship* with Pittsburgh John. Apparently it wasn't much of a relationship. They would talk about what they dreamt and what they said to their analyst and what the analyst said to them. Then they would go out to eat. They smoked a lot. Pall Mall. They didn't drink much. We all went to movies a lot and classes very little.

Pittsburgh John got A's and B pluses. Elise and I got C's and D's and F's and WD (withdrawn) and NC (no credit).

One day, toward evening, I saw Elise wandering through the street.

She didn't seem to see me.

I called her.

She was carrying the Woodie Guthrie record album, 10 inch shellac 78's.

She told me Pittsburgh John had asked her to take the records and not visit for the next few weeks. His girlfriend from Pittsburgh would be in the city. She wouldn't understand.

Elise was broken. She talked to me about their *relationship*, how she wasn't really heartbroken since it wasn't a full adult love-relationship but only a dependency relationship.

She talked on and on.

"Am I boring you?" she asked.

"It's OK," I said.

"Please stay with me tonight," she said. "I don't want to be alone."

I went with her to her room. It was a small furnished room on the top story of a private house, one of those rooms that in "better days" had been the maid's.

"The janitor hasn't given me clean sheets for two weeks," she said. "I haven't paid the rent, so I can't talk to him."

We sat around and talked. I looked at her books. *The Oxford Anthology of Greek Poetry.*

"I stole it from the library," she said.

The Poems of Dylan Thomas.

"I bought it once when I was almost broke," she said. "Whenever I'm almost broke I buy an expensive book."

The Pisan Cantos of Pound.

"I stole that," she said. "I think that's the only moral way to get books."

She talked about her friends. I had thought she knew only Carol and Pittsburgh John. She was part of a circle of poets and psychology students around Columbia. They were all having breakdowns.

She had tried to commit suicide the night before. There were scratches on her wrists. She had also turned on the gas ring for a while.

It was very late.

"Let's get to sleep," I said.

She covered the window with a blanket (she had no shades) and undressed, getting into little-girl pajamas. She washed out her underwear and gargled with an oxygenating rinse. She had trench mouth.

"I'll sleep in the chair," she said. "You can have the bed."

"Shit," I said. "Come on in."

She turned out the light, took the blankets off the window and came to bed.

The next day she got a statement from her analyst that she had to leave Barnard for a while and went back to her parents' home in Washington Heights.

I didn't see her again that term or that summer.

Before the term's end I had had my nervous breakdown and my analyst, a Horneyian on Park Avenue, had given me a note to Columbia telling them I needed a second Senior year. By the time my second Senior year had begun I'd split with my friend David and was onto a second nervous breakdown.

This while working in the juice-pouring and fried egg counter of the Lion's Den in John Jay basement at Columbia.

I was having a nervous breakdown, reading Shakespeare, frying eggs.

One morning (I worked from 8 AM to 10 AM) I looked up. There was only one person in the Lion's Den tables.

It was Elise.

I came over to her.

She was reading Freud (the red-covered Perma-Book edition of the *Introductory Lectures*) and drinking black coffee. She had returned to school. She was studying French. She wanted to read Rimbaud in the original.

She had met, slept with, was in love with a poet. She had worn a red dress the night she met him, had been speechless. He had thought her very deep. Slept with her.

Now she was afraid he would think she was deep.

Where was he now? He was in California with his friend Peter.

I told her about David's defection.

"I'll be getting a room around Columbia," she said. "If things get too bad you can stay with me."

I can only remember one night at her room. It was a furnished room in the private apartment of a Russian woman. The room next to Elise was occupied by a Czech actress called Vera Fusek.

That evening I was terribly depressed over David.

"I think I'm going to commit suicide," I said.

"What's stopping you?" said Elise. She was reading Rimbaud.

"If I wasn't a Catholic I would have committed suicide long ago," said Vera.

The next morning we woke up late and the Russian landlady was already up. Before I left the room Elise made me wear a babushka. I had been wearing blue jeans, a leather jacket, and moccasins. Elise put on her blue jeans (rivets on her fly), her leather jacket, and combat boots. We nodded at the landlady as we left. I, a little conscious of my morning beard.

We got out of Columbia. We all managed somehow. Or we dropped out and went to another school. But we got through. We weren't the type to attend graduation ceremonies and shake hands and pick up diplomas. I can remember finding mine one afternoon, while on my way to the psychiatrist. It was rolled up and in my mailbox at the student dorm. It was dated October 15th. I thought that no one else graduated October 15th. It didn't make me feel boo hoo or ha ha.

Then we were out and drifting in the world.

We began trying to make homes for ourselves. I had the top floor of the house of the sculptor Chaim Gross. It was on West 105th Street. I was moving downtown from Columbia.

Elise had an apartment with Carol. One night I went to visit them.

A tall James Dean looking boy was there. His name was Peter. Elise bare-chested was ironing clothes. Carol was reading *Candide* in the bedroom. Peter was telling us of his first sexual experience, with a Spanish whore.

"Excuse me," he said to me, "I hope you don't mind my asking, but are you homosexual?"

"I don't know yet," I said. "I'm in the middle of my analysis."

"Would you like to sleep with me?" he said.

"Of course," I said. "But it makes me a little nervous to sleep with strangers. I have to go now."

"I hope I haven't offended you," said Peter.

"I'm complimented," I said. "But I have to get up early to go to work."

I left.

I didn't visit Carol and Elise's apartment for a long time after that but I would call, speaking sometimes to Carol, sometimes to Elise, once to Allen who had moved in with them.

Howl had come out. Allen was famous. New York was closing in on him. For a while he and Peter stayed with Carol and Elise. He was getting ready to go to Europe.

I went out with them all one night. We were going to a movie theatre on 42nd Street to see *Vitelloni*. It was the first time I met Allen.

"I went to Columbia," I told him. "After you."

He looked at me. "Columbia ruined a lot of people," he said.

In the movie theatre I was seated beside Peter's brother, Lafcadio.

Vitelloni was on. I saw the city wasn't Rome.

"What city is that?" I asked Laf.

"New York," he said confidently.

Carol and Elise split up right after Allen left for Europe.

I went over to stay with Carol.

She fed me chicken cacciatore. She bought chickens used in the cancer experiments at the Payne Whitney Clinic. They cost only 14c each.

She was looking for a new job. She had no job. Her father was in the hospital dying.

"I lost all respect for her," said Carol.

"Why?" I said.

"When Allen came in she changed completely," said Carol.

"How?" I said.

"Everything she read, said, did, changed," said Carol. "Everything was Allen."

"Don't you like him?" I said.

"He's a slob," she said. "Peter is worth ten of him. Peter is wonderful, so clean, so considerate."

"OK," I said. "I get the picture. Let's get to sleep."

"I am so happy that she's gone!" said Carol.

"OK," I said. "Let's sleep."

In the morning the telephone woke us. It was Carol's stepmother. Carol's father had died.

Carol and I got dressed. We went downstairs.

"Are you going home?" I said.

"I'm going to look for a job," she said.

"But your father just died," I said.

"I still don't have a job," she said.

Her bus came.

Elise had moved to the lower East Side, she and her cat. She suspected the cat of insanity. Elise had been hanging out in a tough lesbian bar. She had an all-night job typing up scripts in a special projection machine for ABC. I had somehow gotten in touch with her. We made a date to meet one evening at the Mariner's Gate, on Central Park West in the Eighties. The Mariner's Gate is one of the entrances to the Park.

She was there and on time. One of the few times she was on time.

She had been kicked out of her job at ABC, literally kicked out. On Friday when she was paid there was a note saying she was suspended. There had been no other notice.

"It's true," she told me. "I was a bad worker. I came in late and often drunk and made many mistakes. But they shouldn't dismiss me with a note. They should come to me personally and say 'Miss Cowen. You stink. Get your ass out of here.' *That* I would have taken."

"What did you do?" I asked.

"I came back Monday and sat at the typing machine. Everyone stared at me. Finally the boss came over. He looked very frightened. He said, 'Miss Cowen, will you leave?' Until then he had always said Elise. If he had even spoken to me in a human way, or called me Elise I would have left. I said, 'I was fired without explanation or discussion. I think I have a right to that. I want to speak to Mr. Lomax, or someone in charge.' He went away. A few minutes later the police came. They grabbed me by the arms and began to pull me away. They didn't even give me a chance to walk normally. When they got me in the door one of the policemen hit me in the stomach, while the others held me. When I got to the police station I called my father. He got in touch with my uncle. They both came down. My father said to me, 'If your mother ever hears of this it will kill her.' "

"Did they lock you up?" I said.

"No," she said. "They let me go. No charges pressed."

"What are you going to do now?"

"I was planning on going to San Francisco," she said. "I'm going to go Wednesday."

We made a date to meet for lunch Tuesday afternoon at the Italian restaurant near my Welfare Training Station on Avenue B and East 3rd Street.

I had gotten a job as Social Investigator for the Welfare Department. I was in training.

But she didn't show up. By Tuesday she had left for California.

There was a real beat scene out on the West coast; I got letters from Elise. She was living with a drunk Irish artist in a cheap rooming house.

One night, lonely for her, I called her. The rooming house said she might be in a bar called The Place. I called The Place. She was there.

"I'm pregnant," she said.

"Can you afford an abortion?"

"They're easier to get out here," she said. "I'll write you from the hospital."

Early in January she wrote me from the hospital. By the time she had qualified for a psychiatric abortion the doctors were all away on Christmas vacation. By the time they returned, after New Year's (she had looked out the window, seen their skis strapped to the auto tops) the foetus had grown too large for a simple C&D. She had to have a hysterectomy.

I sent her a copy of Stendhal's *De l'amour* (in French) to read in the hospital.

"I hope she can get hold of a dictionary," I thought.

Meanwhile time passed. (*Shots of leaves falling. Snow on trees.*) I was working in Welfare, getting a little extra money.

I had made up with David when Columbia ended. He had been in the Navy; now he was out, up in Harvard, getting his Master's.

One weekend I packed to go visit him. As I was about to leave the phone rang.

It was Elise, calling from San Francisco.

"I want back," she said. "Can you send me the money by telegraph?"

"Sure," I said.

I telegraphed the money from Cambridge, Mass.

When she came back to New York City she came to live with me. I was still living in Chaim Gross's house.

We didn't get along.

We had different ideas about what life should be.

I didn't push her to go back to work and Elise was more than a little inhibited about going back, so three months passed. She felt guilty about not getting a job and she made me feel guilty about making her feel guilty. It was very sad.

The whole beat thing seemed sad to me. I didn't mind being poor. But I couldn't stand her idleness, sleeping all day and being so grumpy and saying "and like, and like, and like" all the time and using Negro slang when she was, after all, no Negro at all but a Jewish girl graduated from Barnard.

Peter was back from Europe. He came for dinner one evening with Lafcadio.

I put curry and fried onions into some chopped meat and served it over rice.

We talked about Welfare.

"The Welfare Department wants me to support my mother," said Peter. "Isn't it more important that I save money to go to Japan to worship the Buddha at the Nara Shrine?"

"That's a difficult question," I said.

One evening I told Elise that David would be coming in from Cambridge for the next weekend.

"I'll go to Joyce's," she said.

"You can stay."

"No," she said. "Three's a crowd."

She packed and left.

She called the next Tuesday. She was going to California with Keith Gibbs. She would be by to pick up her belongings and return my hula hoop.

She came by that evening. Keith was waiting downstairs. I helped her bring her things down. She gave me a Marianne Moore record she had stolen from the public library.

We kissed.

"Don't get caught stealing from foreign libraries," I said. "They might send you to the foreign legion with all those Germans."

She went down the stairs.

I heard the car go, made circles with my hula hoop.

I phoned Joyce, talked to her. Joyce said she felt the thing with Keith was *real*, that her love for/with Allen was a dream.

"I don't know," I said.

There were letters from Elise, letters also from Carol. Carol had left for France after her father died. She had a small income. In Paris she had met an Algerian. She was working for Berlitz and the FLN.

I was still working for Welfare. I saved money. I went to Mexico on vacation. I wrote a book, *Leo in Mexico*.

Then Elise was back.

One day the doorbell rang and there she was, holding a bag, just like the movies.

"Don't worry," she said. "I'm not staying. I justed wanted to wash up before going to my parents' house."

Carol had come back from France. The three of us had a party together. I read sections of *Leo in Mexico*; Carol said there would have to be another French Revolution. "Blood has to flow in the streets," she said. She was very pretty. She was wearing a basic black. "What this country needs is a lot of good cheap heroin," said Elise.

Allen had come back. He had moved into 170 East Second Street. He got an apartment for Elise a floor above him. I gave her some of my furniture, furniture my parents had given me, the last of my childhood: cherry-maple furniture. For her house-warming she served peyote buttons and Cosanyl. She wouldn't take the peyote. She had gone too far out the last time. Allen had come in with Peter, talked, left. The man who had helped us move, a young paranoid from California, took one peyote and was AWAY. I ate two. Didn't feel anything.

Elise and I went out walking.

"I'm hungry," I said.

She bought me a plate of spaghetti at Bruno's.

"You're not supposed to be hungry after peyote," she said.

But I was hungry.

From then until the time she died, her world was Allen. When he was interested in Zen, so was she. When he became more interested in Chassidism, so did she. Did he drink mocha coffee? So drank she. When he went down to Peru there was Peter, left behind downstairs, still there to be with. Peter loved a girl from New Jersey. Elise loved the New Jersey girl. When Allen came back, the New Jersey girl moved in with Elise.

New Jersey! New Jersey! I can understand all human passions but how can one love someone from New Jersey!

Then Allen was going to leave again. He was going to India. With Peter. Without Elise.

She came to see me, bringing a salami. Could she stay for a week?

"What happened to your apartment?" I said.

She had given it up.

She was no longer able to do things. She wouldn't/couldn't keep a job, pay rent, electricity. It was too much.

She had been staying at the apartment of Irving Rosenthal but she wanted out.

I lent her $50.

That night she stayed at Carol's new apartment.

She came back the next day, very depressed. Carol had gone rich-girl, waiting for the Revolution in Sutton Place, sharing an apartment with her Aunt. Carpets, over-stuffed furniture, Chinese porcelain.

"I feel she's dead," said Elise.

The next morning she packed her bags to go look for a job. She was wearing toreador pants.

"I don't think you should wear toreador pants for a job interview," I said.

"I'll change in the ladies' room in the subway," she said.

A few days later I got a post card from her. She had gotten a post office box instead of a room. She didn't say where she was living.

I was hospitalized.

The day I got out I went to my post office box. There was my last letter to Elise marked: "Moved. Address unknown."

I called her parents' house.

Elise was in Bellevue. She had gone in with hepatitis (serum), then become psychotic.

"Leo," her mother said, "I want you to be truthful with me. Did Elise ever take drugs?"

"Not to my knowledge," I said.

"Her father looked through her writings while she was in the hospital," she said. "He says they're filthy. She seems to have been mixed up with a lot of homosexuals. Did you notice any among her friends?"

"None," I said. "Can I visit her?"

"She doesn't want any visitors now," Mrs. Cowen said. "Maybe when she gets home."

Carol and I went to see her at her parents' home. Her parents had had her transferred out of Bellevue to a private sanitarium, then signed her out against doctor's orders.

She looked fine, better than we had ever seen her, neat, clean. But she was mad, quite mad. Paranoid. She felt the City (New York City) had machines trained on her, could hear all her thoughts and also that she could hear them, the New York City workers, foolish, bored, boring, mean-souled people. She described to me in detail the four people, two men, two women, assigned to her.

"Elise," I said, "you're paranoid."

"No," she said, "I'm not."

She had become a complete phobic. Always fearful, she couldn't go out any longer without one of her parents.

A child again, and at home.

She had read Joyce's novel *Come and Join the Dance* in which she is given the name of Kay.

"It's *The Group* laid in Barnard," she joked.

She had a review of *The Group* in front of her. I glanced through it. There was a Kay in *The Group*. She became paranoid, had been interned in Bellevue, finally fallen out the window, looking for enemy planes.

"Where are your machines?" I said. "The ones that tap your brain?"

"They plant them outside the window," she said.

Mrs. Cowen had prepared us a supper of slices of tongue heated in the roto broiler. On the side, green peppers and tomatoes she had pickled herself.

We left after supper. I walked with Carol along Overlook Terrace to the subway.

"What do you think?" I said.

Carol sat beside me in the subway. She was distracted. She looked away. I noticed that she wore gloves. Of course. A lady always wears gloves in the street.

Carol sighed in exasperation.

"Leo," she said, "that life seems so far beyond me now. It's unreal. It doesn't make me feel anything."

When we came to her subway stop she got off. "I'll call you," she said.

I wondered why she would call, our worlds now so far apart. . . .

I was working in the Welfare office.

Someone called me to the phone.

DIANE DI PRIMA

The Quarrel

You know I said to Mark that I'm furious at you.

No he said are you bugged. He was drawing Brad who was asleep on the bed.

Yes I said I'm pretty god damned bugged. I sat down by the fire and stuck my feet out to warm them up.

Jesus I thought you think it's so easy. There you sit innocence personified. I didn't say anything else to him.

You know I thought I've got work to do too sometimes. In fact I probably have just as fucking much work to do as you do. A piece of wood fell out of the fire and I poked it back in with my toe.

I am sick I said to the woodpile of doing dishes. I am just as lazy as you. Maybe lazier. The toe of my shoe was scorched from the fire and I rubbed it where the suede was gone.

Just because I happen to be a chick I thought.

Mark finished one drawing and looked at it. Then he put it down and started another one.

It's damned arrogant of you I thought to assume that only you have things to do. Especially tonight.

And what a god damned concession it was for me to bother to tell you that I was bugged at all I said to the back of his neck. I didn't say it out loud.

I got up and went into the kitchen to do the dishes. And shit I thought I probably won't bother again. But I'll get bugged and not bother to tell you and after a while everything will be awful and I'll never say anything because it's so fucking uncool to talk about it. And that I thought will be that and what a shame.

Hey hon Mark yelled at me from the living room. It says here Picasso produces fourteen hours a day.

[1961]

Requiem

I think
you'll find
a coffin
not so good
Baby-O.
They strap you in
pretty tight

I hear
it's cold
and worms and things
are there for selfish reasons

I think
you'll want
to turn
onto your side
your hair
won't like
to stay in place
forever
and your hands
won't like it
crossed
like that

I think
your lips
won't like it
by themselves

Minor Arcana

Body
whose flesh
has crossed my will?
Which night
common or blest
shapes now
to walk the earth?

Body
whose hands
broke ground
for that thrusting head?
in the eyes
budding to sight
who will I read?

Body
secret in you
sprang this cry of flesh

Now tell the tale

The Window

you are my bread
and the hairline
noise
of my bones
you are almost
the sea

you are not stone
or molten sound
I think
you have no hands

this kind of bird flies backward
and this love
breaks on a windowpane
where no light talks

this is not time
for crossing tongues
(the sand here
never shifts)

I think
tomorrow
turned you with his toe
and you will
shine
and shine
unspent and underground

For Zella, Painting

1

what are you.
thinking.
at night/these nights/night
when
(unsleeping)
the red.
the hills
where you walk.

and who could tolerate that sky.

2

what blue is that
your eyes
your lumpy shirt

while you.
stand.
slumping in dawn light
(same blue)

and from your hands the cadmiums run, shouting.

from Memoirs of a Beatnik

Then one day I wandered into the Quixote Bookstore on MacDougal Street and Norman Verne, the proprietor, offered me a job: he and his wife Gypsy wanted to go canoeing on the Canadian lakes for a month, and would I like to manage the store? The store came with a kitchen in the back, complete with stove and refrigerator, and there was an army cot to set up in the middle of the back room, where one could sleep in comparative luxury. The rains and thunderstorms of late August had begun, and the park was neither as pleasant nor as convenient as it had been, so I accepted, gave a few days' notice to all my painters, and moved in, attaché case and all, and Norm and Gypsy took off.

After they were gone, I discovered that the store also came with its own built-in junkie: a very beautiful, ghostlike blonde boy named Luke Taylor, who played a very heavy shade blues guitar and shot a lot of heroin—"horse" as we called it then. I had seen Luke around the scene for some time—he used to frequent the Saturday night "rent parties" that were held in a loft around Twentieth Street and Seventh Avenue—and I had eyes for him from the first time I heard him sing. Something about the supercool, wasted look: the flattened, broken nose, the drooping green eyes, thin pinched junkie face with its drawn mouth—the mixture of hungry and bitter—cut right through me, and left me wanting to touch, to fondle, to somehow warm that chilly flesh. I was in love with Luke then, and for some time to come.

On the first night that I was taking care of the store—it opened around four in the afternoon and stayed open till midnight in order to cover the tourist trade—I was standing in the doorway, looking out at the scene on MacDougal Street. The Village had gotten tougher as the summer had worn on. It was one of those years in the middle of the nineteen-fifties when the Italians who lived below Bleecker Street, getting more and more uptight behind the huge influx of "new Bohemians" (the word "beatnik" had not yet been coined) were beginning to retaliate with raids and forays into what we had traditionally considered our territory: the streets north of Bleecker. On their side, it must be admitted that we were invading, moving into their turf *en masse*. Many new apartments on Sullivan Street, Thompson Street, etc., had been opened up to us by the real estate moguls. They were cheap, convenient to the Village scene, and in the heart of the Italian neighborhood. Into them flocked unheeding the boys and girls of the new Village: men who wore sandals, or went barefoot, and sometimes wore jewelry, girls who favored heavy eye makeup and lived with a variety of men, outright faggots, and—worst crime of all to the Italian slum mind—racially mixed couples.

The police were run by Tammany Hall, and Tammany was itself the heart of the Italian Village, and so they tended to ignore the escapades of the Italian youth. Only two days before, I had stood in Washington Square and watched a police car cruise slowly up the block and away, while about twenty young men pursued François, a quiet, pale-skinned mulatto boy from the Bahamas, into a building then under construction. The twenty hoodlums milled about in the empty lot next door, shouting obscenities and afraid to enter the building, till someone started, and they all took up the chant "Get a pipe! Get a pipe!" The police car pulled smoothly away to the tune of this bloodthirsty chant, with never a backward glance. François, whom I knew slightly, had been making it with Linda, a pretty white chick of about sixteen, since he hit the Village at the beginning of the summer.

On this particular evening, I stood on the steps of my new store and watched three young faggots get beaten up by their dago brothers. A not unusual evening's entertainment. A cool breeze was coming up and many people were out enjoying the soft summer air. The young men ducked into a hallway two doors away from me. Scuffling and screams. The police pulled up. They bravely entered the building, arrested the three gay men and drove away. About three minutes later, the young gangsters emerged from the building and continued their stroll up the block.

Somebody came into the shop and asked for *Vestal Lady on Brattle*, Gregory Corso's first book, which had just been printed in Cambridge. There was no "beat poetry" as yet, it was just another poetry book. After the customer left, I settled down on the stoop to read a copy. I was deep into Gregory's peculiarly beautiful head when Luke appeared, guitar in hand.

"Where's Norm?" he asked hoarsely. His voice was always hoarse, was hardly more than a whisper, with that peculiar junk roughness.

"He's gone," I said, "for four weeks. Gone camping with Gypsy in Canada."

Luke muttered some obscenity, started to take off, then came back and sat down beside me on the metal steps.

"You watching the store?" he asked.

I nodded.

"You gonna be sleeping here?" he persisted, edging toward the thing that was on his mind.

I nodded again. Supercool, me too.

"Oh," he said. He was silent for a few minutes, and we both watched the street.

Then he said, "I was living in back here. Didn't Norm tell you?"

Now, Norm had told me nothing—whether because he wanted to cool the scene with Luke and was hoping I would get rid of him, or for whatever reasons of his own, I didn't know.

"No," I said. I was quite surprised. One of the things I had really been looking forward to was having that combination kitchen-bedroom all to myself, and cooking little things, and puttering, and playing the hi-fi: playing house, for all the world as if it were mine, and mine alone. After you've been on the streets for a while, living alone becomes the ultimate luxury.

I was quiet, but Luke, I was sure, could hear me thinking, with that telepathy people develop when they are continually at the mercy of others. I glanced sidelong at him and my heart went out to him. I wanted to touch those long, skinny, dirty fingers—beautifully articulate hands with the mercilessly bitten nails. A pang of desire shot like lightning through my groin.

"No, I didn't know you were staying here," I said softly, "but if you want to, I guess you still can. I mean—we can figure something out so we both fit." I didn't look at him. "Why don't you go on back and stash your guitar?"

"Yeah," he said, and I met his eyes, and he flashed a smile. "Yeah, thanks. All I want to do right now is fall out."

I went back with him, and helped him set up the cot, and he flung himself across it, declining blankets and food, and in a moment was deeply asleep.

The street got dark, a few people came and bought books. I read the rest of *Vestal Lady on Brattle*, but all the while my head was in the back room with Luke, anticipating the night. I felt as if someone had laid a rare gift in my hands.

At last it was midnight and I locked the front door and turned out the lights in the front of the store. I poked my head in back and Luke was still sound asleep, so I decided to go out for a while and ramble. The street was extraordinarily quiet and, after checking out the scene at Rienzi's and the Limelight, I realized that I hadn't eaten supper and was very hungry, and that Luke would probably be hungry too when he woke up. There was a deli on Seventh Avenue that was open all night, and there I bought frozen potato pancakes and jars of apple sauce and cokes for a late meal.

When I got back to the store on MacDougal Street it was about three in the morning. I let myself in and groped my way to the narrow back room without turning any lights on. I found the refrigerator and stuck the bag of groceries in without unpacking it. The light from inside fell across Luke's face, and he stirred and half-opened his eyes. He had been up for a while, I figured, because the amplifier of the hi-fi set was glowing orange in the dark. I switched it off, and slipped out of my clothes, terribly aware of Luke, awake and silent in the dark.

I found a blanket, wrapped myself in it, and lay down beside him on the cot, feeling him move over slightly to make room for me, feeling his hard, tense body next to mine in the dark, his clothes and my blanket between us. He reached out and traced my face and neck in the dark, ending with a brotherly squeeze of my shoulder.

"You OK?" he mumbled. "You got enough room? 'Cause I can sleep on the floor."

"No," I said, "I'm fine. You?"

"OK," he whispered. "I'm just OK, I guess." I could sense his smile in the dark.

I must have dozed off, because when I opened my eyes again it was light with the grey light of pre-dawn and Luke, stretched on his side, leaning on his elbow, his chin in his hand, looked down on me.

He smiled when I opened my eyes.

"Can't you sleep?" I asked him.

"Slept enough, I guess," and he bent down, and I reached up, and we found ourselves kissing.

My shyness with Luke—the shyness that always comes over me when I really have eyes for someone—had disappeared while I slept. Our kiss went on and on, and it seemed to me that the darkness had returned, and my hands fumbled in the dark to remove the clothes that hid that lean, tense body from me. He was wearing a red and black flannel work shirt, and I unbuttoned it blindly and slipped it off him licking and kissing at his chest. But when I started on the zipper of his fly, he caught my hands and held them still.

"Hey," he said gently, "hey." He unwound the blanket that was wrapped around me, brushed the hair out of my eyes, and began to nuzzle my breasts and stroke my sides.

I looked down at the thin dirty fingers on my shoulder, and they were trembling. I covered them with my own and drew them down to my breast, holding them with a warm steady pressure till the trembling stopped, and then drawing his hand on down to my cunt. His fingers closed over it, pressing clit and opening, but did not enter, and I was left in the grip of a warm, sickly feeling of desire alleviated but not satisfied. I slid my hands around his shoulders and drew him down to me, kissing him again and again on that thin, hungry mouth, drinking the bitterness and hurt, the sickly taste of endless lonely junksick mornings, the anger and coldness that translated as containment, or shyness.

His hand tightened over my cunt and the other slipped around and under my waist and held me close. I kissed his eyelids, the skin under his closed eyes, the bridge of his nose. Suckled at his eyebrows, smoothing his temples and the hollows of his gaunt cheeks with my lips. My hands slipped down inside his jeans, and he let go of me long enough to slip out of them, so that my palms curved concave against the hollows in his lean buttocks. My right hand slid down, one finger sunk deep into his asshole, the others stroking the skin behind his balls. I could feel his cock grow still larger against the soft flesh of my stomach. My cunt convulsed in a spasm that left me moist and aching with desire.

Luke's hand stirred against me, and he thrust two fingers deep into my wet cunt with long, sure strokes, moving slow and heavy as the blues he played. A moan escaped me, and I began to move in the preliminary rhythms of orgasm, but I wanted to prolong this moment, to suck the juice and essence, the very marrow and soul of this man I had wanted for so long. And so I shifted slightly, almost imperceptibly, my mounting excitement lost a bit of its edge, the mists cleared momentarily.

My finger in his asshole began to rotate slowly, moving in larger and larger circles, and the fingers that were stroking him found his balls and caressed them with a touch infinitely light and tender. I slid my free hand between my stomach and his, and closed my fingers over his cock. I felt as if I were fainting.

A feeling of utter surrender swept over me, I knew I belonged to him totally, to his hunger and darkness and magic. I wanted him to mark me permanently with some mark that proclaimed me his, to enter all of my orifices at once, to leave me utterly used, spent, exhausted as I had never been, while I felt peace grow in him at last, and I became the ground devoured to feed and suckle the small, deeply buried seed of his joyousness. All of my flesh seemed to melt, to grow into his, as my hand moved up and down on his huge, stiff cock, and he, divining something of my thoughts, set his teeth against my shoulder and drew blood, with a pain that was ecstasy itself.

Then he moved above me, I threw my two legs over his shoulders as his hands on my shoulders drew me against him, and I could feel the walls of my cunt stretch taut to contain the huge cock which filled me to the bursting. I could hardly bear it, and my cries of pain and ecstasy filled the small, littered room, my head rolled from side to side on the small cot, and my hands on his buttocks drew him to me again and again as he lunged with fierce, searing strokes that seemed to penetrate the very core of my being. When I came, in a great, bursting flood of light, I felt as if I must literally die, that my flesh could not possibly contain the current that was flowing through it, and I heard a voice that I realized must be my own filling the room with short, stabbing animal cries as I slipped into darkness.

The roar of the waves slowly receded, leaving me high and dry on a white beach, in a blinding white light. I opened my eyes and met Luke's slanting green ones, glazed and distant. I watched for a long time while the glint of human consciousness slowly returned to them. His lips moved dimly. "God," he said hoarsely, in his indistinct undertone. "God, I think I love you."

"Hush," I said, "hush," pulling his head against my breast. For to name it was to make it less than it was.

We lay together for a long time without moving again. In vain did the sunshine pour into the sordid little room, insisting that it was day, that this was the dusty, cluttered back room of a Village bookstore, that we were, in fact, two rather young, rather vulnerable human creatures on an uncomfortable army cot. We two were one seed form, one kernel, nested in darkness, in hard shell, dark and smooth inside, whose downy exterior cushioned us from sound and motion. We two, one seed form, nestled closed and together in our own germinating warmth till the long fingers of light and wind should find us and coax us back into being.

"Pre-matter energy," I thought dreamily, thinking of Reich, and realized I had been touched at last, had been truly entered, that there was a dark core of mystery in our coming together that I would never penetrate.

We lay there together as long as we could, at first oblivious to everything but each other, and then later trying not to be moved by the noises of the traffic, the bustle of the outside, the increasingly warm sun that was pouring in through the back window of the shop. We were hungry and we had to go to the bathroom, but every time one of us moved an experimental limb the other would clasp him (or her) tighter and nestle closer.

Finally hunger won the day, and with one quick movement I slid out of Luke's arms, stood up, and made for the refrigerator with its stash of goodies. I put up a pot of coffee, and was just opening the package of frozen potato pancakes, cutting into the brightly colored plastic wrapper with the point of a paring knife, when Luke came up behind me and put his arms around my waist, and I could feel his hard, full cock jabbing at my buttocks. He said nothing, just pulled me close and hard up against him with those lean tense arms of his, and tried to get his cock in between the two mounds of my ass, into my asshole.

I went limp at his touch, melted up against him, fitting my body to his, and when I sensed what he wanted I bent at the waist, leaning over the table to help him get in. But I was too tight, and he drew me away from the table, and the next thing I knew I was lying face down on the floor, spread-eagled with Luke straddling me. He must have reached the cooking oil down from the table, for his hands, covered with oil, were all over my ass and into my asshole. As his lean, powerful fingers entered my anus, I cried out, I nearly fainted with a pleasure that was at the same time an unappeasable longing, an aching desire that I felt somehow could never be satisfied. Then his hands tugged at me, raising my haunches as his big, full cock entered me. He lay full length on me, his hand on my cunt, pressing into the hard, gritty floor, his thin mouth sucking and nipping at my shoulders.

When I first hit the ground I had put my hands under my head to cushion my face, protect it from the dirty floorboards, but my desire to touch him, to caress him any way I could, was too much for me, and, even as I was pounded, ground into the worn linoleum by the rapidly increasing rhythms of his lust, my hands came around and stroked and caressed his sides, his buttocks, and my feet came up to stroke his thin, muscular legs.

There was a blindness to his passion that set up a momentary resistance in me. I was being used as I had never been used, and I was not sure that I liked it, could rise to meet this demand; but the tremulous insistence of his hand in my cunt—through the wall of which, I knew, he could feel his cock pulsing and lunging in my ass—and the blind force of his passion, breaking through his flesh and tangling with his mouth in my hair, cut through all thought, and I heard myself crying out that he should never stop, and then crying again and again in a wordless rage of pain and pleasure that was a hymn of praise to the light of ecstasy exploding in us both.

I got off the floor, dirty, disheveled and bruised, and with oil on my ass, and went on with the business of preparing breakfast. Or whatever meal it was. The sun, it seemed, was going down. The store hadn't been opened. Some semblance of responsibility led me now to throw a trench coat around myself and tape a scribbled note to the front door: "Sorry, Closed Today. Will Open Tomorrow As Usual." I puttered a while, straightening up the store, and went back again to the back room in the dusk now, and found Luke nodding out at the table, a towel around his waist, having turned on in the hall john, and my heart sank a little, but I said nothing; instead I put the "Carmina Burana" on the hi-fi, but soft, and sat down with Hesse's *Demian* to read a little. In those days Hesse had not been reprinted, was in English only in an early, out-of-print edition, and was eagerly seized upon whenever it turned up. It got dark. I switched on a lamp, brewed a pot of coffee, and switched from Carl Orff to the Modern Jazz Quartet, "Django."

After a while Luke stirred, and I gave him some coffee without saying anything, not knowing where he was at, or if he wanted to talk, and he drank it, watching me over the cup while I sat reading, or pretending to read, till I heard his gruff, half-pleading "Come here," and went to him immediately, kneeling by his chair, my head in his lap, while he stroked my hair, wordless, and I finally turned my head and untied his silly little towel and found his cock with my lips. And slowly, slowly, under the long, gentle ministrations of my mouth and tongue it grew hard, and in the slow, hot, summer night with all the noises of August backyards and August streets exploding around us, I made love to that thick, strong, uncircumcised cock, made love indeed, called love into being, coaxed it into fullness and feeling with my mouth—I was young enough and had magic enough to do that. In love, I MADE love, and love flowered like a aureole around us both, and my mouth moved slowly, endlessly, tirelessly, slipping and plunging on that thick, full member, till it began to buck and press against my palate like some wild and eager bird seeking freedom, and I moved faster and faster, and a great sigh that was the lifebreath itself escaped from Luke, and I drank in his seed, drank in his bitter, crystal seed in great eager gulps, as if to bring us together finally and for all time, so that no change, nothing and no one, could put us apart again. My hands were on his fine, thin waist as he came, I could feel his back arch, the electricity in his flesh, and my head between his strong, golden-haired thighs was clasped tightly, I could hear his blood—or my own—exploding in my ears, and knew this seed I swallowed for the sacrament—the holy and illimitable essence that drove the stars.

Then he bent and kissed my mouth to taste himself, and we sat for a long time in the summer night, my hair tumbled over his lap, his hands cupping my shoulders. When at last we groped our way back to our cot and slept, it was the wondering and joyous sleep of children on Christmas eve; we kept waking up and touching each other, simply to taste the magic.

BRENDA FRAZER

Breaking out of D.C. (1959)

If I thought he'd listen, I'd say, "Don't go!" The spiraling lift of emotions, he's here one day then gone, we're married only three weeks after we meet and then he drives away, leaving with voices that interrupt our life, shouting up to him from the street, he looks out the balcony window. But my words fail, my voice hangs just short of speech, thinking he must know how I feel. No wonder I'm lonely. "C'mon Babe, don't be that way." "But I feel so trapped!" His friends come loudly up the steps to my apartment and he says to them, "That's my ol' lady, but don't even look at her!" They laugh and look at me in awe, a poet's wife, who would've thought? "Thighs like you've never seen before, and never will see since," he says. I'm quiet and so they continue making their plans about the trip to New York. Their talk is like single-celled animals, amoeba under glass, bumping each other, patting each other on the back in the galactic pond. I'm the only serious one, going into my low cycle that prepares the heart for pain, closing everything off except for secret messages like this, low singing under my breath, inside ear echoing, who's to notice?

He's on his way home, really it's Jersey City, New York, what's the difference. The poetry reading that brought him here to D.C. was our meeting place. Now I guess I'm staying here, thinking how moments ago we were so close to talking, before his friends arrived. "Let's talk," he said, as he sat cross-legged on the barewood floor, the whole night ahead of us, the park across the street, the federal buildings of the U.S. government looming all around my 13th Street house that would probably be steelballed soon. "I like your quietness, you know," and holds me close to ease the hurt. "Other women talk too much and it's meaningless. I can hear things in your silence." And later he said, "Quiet people are usually writers." I'm thinking I will be whatever he is, whatever he wants me to be. Mortal practice, a life/death pact to come of this spontaneous knowledge.

They smoke a joint. It goes round to me. "Love's our religion, it's holy, man." He gasps the smoke in, his arm around my shoulder as I lean forward giggling, the floor is covered with old cigarette butts and cans.

"But our system kills it, you know. Kills it and eats it for lunch like sandwich meat, our wounded heart!" "Yeah man, that's right," one of them says, learning from Ray already.

Some of these friends of his are poets, some have cars, or grass, or money, some are just friends. They seem to manifest these relations from the momentary scene, the cosmic vibrations interdependent, you lose your wallet, I find it, someone starves, another finds a job, unwilling. Showers of gold sunbeam energy stronger than normal influences transmute to compassion and send them looking for communication, streets, telephones, getting high. And once in awhile I say something when we're all tuned in and it's so much funnier than I thought, and they break up and it's momentarily ok because they love Ray and me too. And now they're leaving me behind while they take Ray off to New York, ironic.

Now they're all gone and my mood is irritable. The buzz of thoughts like an ache that won't let go. So painful. "Don't say you love me and then leave me behind!" I should have said it. "I'm not hurting you Babe you're *getting* hurt," he would've said. My mental conversation becomes bluesy. "If you love your woman, take her everywhere you go. Let her see what you see and don't ever leave her waiting . . ." Door, waiting at the door, at the window? Will I wait?

"You're not paying attention honey. You ain't high or somethin are you?" Maggie sits facing me, our typewriters back to back between us. I tell her I can't concentrate, my husband went back to New York last night. It's the third time I've had to redo this letter. I like this woman very much. One nice thing about the government jobs is that there are lots of black people. But I can't escape her notice, and the piles of work beside me, no place to hide, not even in my dreaming where I'm marching slowly ahead of the sun, secure in my vow to Ray. The night was spent in dark sleeplessness and now I'm deciding things in a moment that probably require careful thought. "Maybe I won't go home for lunch today," I say to the room in general. "Maybe I'll work straight through and leave early." Maggie and the other women there are supportive of me I know. Just a few days ago they gave me a party when they found out I was married. The gift of a crystal candy dish Ray used for chips with our beercan drinks. "Yeah, honey, go get your man, that's the important thing," says Maggie.

Later I call Myrna Coven's apartment. The phone is busy so I know she's there and go. You couldn't really call it a social visit because I don't like her, memories of the poetry reading when Ray was choosing between us. But then I don't want to go back to my apartment either. I hope to run into Giltbloom there, he usually shows up with some weed every night. "I just got home from work," she says, and I wonder where she can work with her eyes painted so black and pale blond makeup on the pink face? She's looking at me too and does a charcoal sketch of me while we're sitting there. Maybe she thinks she's an artist. I get really offended when I see the picture, her rendition of my skull-short hair and navy surplus sweater. "You're so lucky to be married to Ray. Will you live in New York?" she asks. I forget to tell her that Ray's gone. Finally we hear Giltbloom's motorcycle outside, and he comes in cata-lysing everything, making things happen as he always does. "I've got some pot," he says, smiling at me. He doesn't ask about Ray and I'm glad.

We're all part of D.C.'s growing artists' scene. Giltbloom knows a lot about it because he gets around with the grass. I'm thinking how many more of these people I know since the poetry reading. Even now though I'm shy and only communicate with intuitive skills, sincerity in the eyes and heart, the sense of friends expands now that I have Ray. It's like we all mix in an elemental way, growing with connections, vibrating like leaves on a tree. We're smoking now and I'm wondering how to get Giltbloom to help me without thinking I'm using him to get back to Ray.

Giltbloom already has the plan for the night. We'll go to the Carousel Jazz Club on North Capitol Street. So Myrna and the others take a cab while I'm on the bike with Giltbloom for the thrills. We all arrive together, piling out of cabs and off cars where some are waiting for us. We get introduced. "This is Bonnie, Ray's wife." Socially self-conscious we stand around a little silly on the sidewalk in front of the club, counting our money. There's me, Giltbloom, Eddie Nile and the young paintress he is courting. I know he would normally take any woman he wants without preliminary, but Lorna is rich and gets special treatment. Eddie suffers under the imposition, his gentle thief's honor causes him to speak complaints to anyone who'll listen, softly putting her down. "Eddie's a second story man," Giltbloom told me before, and I think of Ray's convict life. Myrna and a bunch of other art students are in the company too. As we go in Giltbloom stops at the cigarette machine, his brand, we smoke together at the table, his friendly come-on, respectful, which he withholds, creates a pleasant tension.

A small raised stage right next to us, the bass fiddle horizontal on the floor almost touches my leg which I've propped up on the stage for comfort. The red entrance curtains cover the wall next to the stage too and brush against my back with nightclub aesthetic. We drink one round of beers for a very long while. The bass player arrives and hands up his instrument in the colorful lights, no mistakes in his playing even when he sweats, blue dripping on the metal strings, making the fingers slide. The carousel spins like a piloted stage, sinks to the low-down internal atmosphere, the bowed level of the bass. "Someone buzzing like a bee," the audience responds. Betty Carter comes to the stage, in a dress of metallic lamé color, her mouth open to sing, sound and color mix, the first notes visible in cheeks and teeth and inside lower lip warbling to slide out solid in the air. The bass rips apart the patterns and then she steps up on it atop the tempo and spreads arms to fly, spouting, spewing long twirling lines of song, she sings so hard her dress changes color.

After that we sit with our long finished beers watching some traveling magician perform. Maybe we'll wait for the next show, two hours? The music and lights remind me of my red light bedroom with Ray there yesterday. The music full-blast on the old phonograph, Coltrane breathless, I'm flexible cross-legged on Ray's lap in yab-yum embrace while he touches my back in patterns of the bass. Giltbloom's watching me. "I want to go to New York," I say, almost crying. "I know," he says, "I can see that. But when?" "Now, tonight, that's all," emphatically. "But I don't have any money," he laughs. "And me neither," I say giggling at our empty beer glasses. "Wait here a minute, maybe Eddie's girl will want to pick up something," and I'm watching for him as five minutes later he's back and with a nod to the others we leave.

We leave D.C. at night, the late west moon another light on the Capitol dome behind us. Scenery reflects in the blue windshield, I'm watching over Giltbloom's shoulder. The cockeyed slow lifting plane, the flying saucer perspective of north D.C. and the Carousel Club and friends, my apartment, belongings, job all left behind.

In Delaware at dawn we get breakfast in a touristy bus station with turnstiles and a cafeteria. The long night in my bones, already had to stop once before dawn, he'd made me walk to get the circulation going. "We'll go backroad ways now," he said, "so we can stop more often." The *New York Times* spread out on the restaurant table. "We are the responsible generation," he tells me. A bus comes in and tourists line up. Our toast and bacon breakfast enough, we leave. Across the road from the station a farmhouse with peculiar whiteness in the dawn. A dog out back on a chain. The strange simplicity of window casements and house in fine outline of white catches the sun. Giltbloom is young, my age, nineteen, tall and blond, his beak face forceful.

Into Pennsylvania, we're bounding hills of side road, even the ditches are hilly and dangerous and I'm getting dizzy. It gets to be afternoon and we're still negotiating traffic circles on the truck route U.S. 1, the slow motion and frustrated delay. Stop beneath a billboard to rest awhile. He goes to call Ray and I sleep. Sunny fantasies of Giltbloom, I dream, my leg stretched out, reaching, the bass alongside horizontal like last night, only now it's in warm sunlight. Giltbloom wakes me irritated. "Ray's pissed," he says. "I should've known."

Jersey City, Railroad Avenue, Ray's mother's house, philodendron pots have my attention. Has he told her yet that we're married? "You just don't understand how it is!" he's telling me. "It's not so simple, getting out of jail, there's the parole officer to deal with. I have to be cool you know? I'm not supposed to be out of New Jersey." And so I'm figuring out now that he expected me to stay in D.C. while he lived here. And yet what about all the poetry readings in New York? "But see Babe, they can't know that we're married, that's all, or I'll go back to jail!" I'm thinking that my fears are more fundamental than his and though the foreign atmosphere of this place, the tenements, the clotheslines from fire escapes is a shock to me, I know I can't go back. "I'm staying," I say, and "I'm not going back. They can take my belongings from my apartment, my chest of stuff, my violin and my pots and pans and throw it all in the garbage. I'm here to stay. So figure it out!" For once he has no words and just looks at me, his thin eyebrows high over the Pisces eyes I want to touch with soothing cool water, now raised with surprise. I think they're telling me, "You can't do that."

SANDRA HOCHMAN

Farewell Poems

You never saw my rib cage. I would lie next to you
Breathing and my ribs would hardly be visible but
They would be there, shiny under the moon, the polished
Bones, and I would watch them go up and down but you
Would not see them. You were off somewhere else dreaming
Of what would be, dreaming of alarms or the slow waking
Of the next day. I don't know what you were dreaming
But blatant as horns in the dream were my questions.

I was sleeping next to you. Fluids
Of my body were endless as ferns.
I contained the ocean and the river bed. I slept
Without waking. And when I woke I heard the snow
Outside the window.
What were we doing?

We were sleeping. Our legs touched.
But you never looked at my arms. You never saw my arms. I had
Hidden them skillfully under a long robe during the daytime
And I had used them to carry baskets and books and flowers
In great brick pots. I had been housekeeping and
Then, before sleep, I rubbed the petals on my palms. And
Watched the endless snow fall down. Crystals in the dark and
I wanted to give you the gift of my very cold arms.

About My Life at That Time

If I was a huntress of words
It was because I was a huntress of silence,

And just as the Indians went out to trap
Otter, jackal, swollen pelts of beasts,

So I went trapping silence for myself.

At night I listened
To the fumes, the greased machines,
The end of things.

When a wheel broke, it was not the wheel of life,
Buddha's great wheel of birth and endless death,
It was the pierced flat tire of the car
Dying beneath the windows.

Silence was always close to me:
That moment when I move inside the dream
To pierce things.

Postscript

I gave my life to learning how to live.
Now that I have organized it all, now that
I have finally found out how to keep my clothes
In order, when to wash and when to sew, how
To control my glands and horny moments,
How to raise a family, which friends to get
Rid of and which to be loyal to, who is
Phony and who is true, how to get rid of
Ambition and how to be thrifty, now that I have
Finally learned how to take off the mask
And be nude in my secret silence,
This life is just about over.

Julian

I bought white corduroy slacks, which I'm still wearing,
And in that waxed sun afternoon we went sailing, went
On that spinnaker sea—beyond the sagging wharf,
Out of the distant coast—to that far place where no one
Comes—

And we talked about Japan, about shells, about dreaming
As we steered to a world as clean as a girl's drawing. It
Was brighter than blue crayon on that sea, on that sea
Of inspired designs, on that place of endless crystals,
Endless time, endless eels and sea-bugs, grammar
Of the gulled life. Julian, you were in your prime!

Once upon a time I told you, "Take those wooden shoehorns
Out of all your shoes, Julian, you're too neat!" You shot back,
"Mind your own *business*, Miss Beatnik, if you're so free
Why don't you move out of your father's maid's room and live
On your own?" That settled it.

Remembering all your presents, phone calls—
You'd call to go out for a walk—I place you back,
In my imagination—When we walk
Through Central Park and watch the end
Of summer kites bob in the sky. "Life is floating from us,"
I hear you say. I am astonished to hear about
Novels, pencils, paintings, pebbles—You know everything—
Honest man, curious, observant, pushing us all
Into the forbidden places of kindness, you are always
Lonely. And true. You know so much we can learn from! But.

On this morning, I center on death. And the serenity
Of a cold country without you.

The Seed

I was in the blushberries,
Grapes and muscadines,
Peaches and ripe nectarines,
Making salads out of cucumbers,
Grafting seedlings and rootstocks,
Planting onions beside lilac
And grafting new life in the stalk.

I was cooking red tomatoes,
Pods of snap beans, winding
Garlic branches in my hands.

I see you weeping in the hospital. Are
Your arms thin as a carrot?
You do not have to tell me about death—
Onions replace the heart, beet blood
Around the mouth, mud
Spooned out of his thighs,
Bowels in the daybed sheets—
Death spreads as quickly as the seed.

Cancer

I would like to see what it
Looks like. Is it a mirror?
Or a lump of something?
Or a weed? I want to see
It naked and not be afraid.

I sit on a table
Looking at my body,
Waiting for Dr. Fells to come
Back in the room. His air
Conditioner blurs out the
Noise of other people on
West End Avenue living
In their apartments, boxing
With their shadows.

The body a treasure to squander: the
Soldiers in Asia who will
Not fight. "They refuse to
Move, sir," goes through my
Mind.

The air conditioner
Gunning around and around
Is sucking in my list of
Symptoms, taking my
Secret affairs and dumping
Them out the window, distributing
Them on top of people's heads.

His other window faces on
A courtyard. Once in those
Courtyards clothespickers cried
From West End Avenue
To the Drive, singing,
"I cash clothes," and
In those courtyards
Beggars once arrived
As I dropped them pennies
Wrapped in
Dishrags. "I want to be

A minstrel," I confided
To my grandmother. "I want
To sing in courtyards."

Now, high above a courtyard,
I relieve myself of my body
On a doctor's table. I tell
Him my own story.

Burning with Mist
In memory of Lily Cushing

All that I wanted
When I once wanted everything
Was this: To be
Allowed to name things.

To discover, like Noah,
The name of each animal,
Saying each name
As if I had invented it—

Each word excites me. I enter into
Names.

Find me in the lists of
All things, in the names
Of berries, nuts, holly.
To turn lists into
Songs is holy.

But more than names—I
Have become that force
Inside the lily in the flush of growth,
Entering the garden, bulb,
Blossom, and shoot,
Untangling myself at the root.

There Are No Limits to My System

Afterwards,
Clean my body as if it were
A room.

Polish my nails
With lemon oil—
Rub my eyes with
Scouring powder. The
Eyes are made of
Marble.

My tears: tap water.
Clean my body, toes
And fingers. Make me
Wholly insensitive
To pine.

I am olive-skinned
And please do not disturb
Me. Maid, make up the
Room. The rabbis have
Gazed fondly upon me.
The doctors have opened and
Closed my doors. The
Simple friends have
Come in and out of my brain
Like sunspots.

Death
Reduces
Me instantly
To this:
A body.
A whore-poet
In an
Old
Quiet
Room.

JOYCE JOHNSON

from **Minor Characters**

I moved out of 116th Street on Independence Day, 1955—a date I'd chosen not for its symbolism but because it was the first day of a long weekend. I'd taken a tiny maid's room in an apartment on Amsterdam Avenue five blocks away, to which I planned to move all my things, going back and forth with my mother's shopping cart.

I got up early that morning and started putting books into shopping bags. When I thought my parents would be awake, I walked into their room. They were dozing in their twin beds, an oscillating fan whirring between them. I said, "I have something to tell you. I'm moving out today." I felt sick to my stomach, as if I had murdered these two mild people. I could see their blood on the beige summer covers.

Two weeks earlier I'd found the room. With the first paychecks from my new job, I'd bought an unpainted rocking chair, a small desk, two sheets, and a poster of Picasso's *Blue Boy*—the furnishings of my first freedom. I knew children did not own furniture.

All this had been accomplished in secret, like the arrangements for a coup d'état. I wouldn't speak until it was time to leave. There was nothing to discuss. I was terribly afraid of being talked out of it.

"I need to borrow the cart," I said to my mother, "for my clothes and books."

"Don't think—" she said. "Don't think you can just come around here for dinner any time you want."

All day long I dragged the cart back and forth over the hot red brick sidewalks of the Columbia campus. No one shouted. No one stood at the door on 116th Street and tried to bar my way. In the stillness of their house, my parents moved slowly around the rooms as if injured.

I was done by evening. On my way out for the last time, I wrote my address on a piece of paper and left it on the kitchen table. From my new apartment, I called Elise and Sheila, who were sharing a place in Yorkville. "I really did it, I guess," I said.

Everyone knew in the 1950s why a girl from a nice family left home. The meaning of her theft of herself from her parents was clear to all— as well as what she'd be up to in that room of her own.

On 116th Street the superintendent knew it. He'd seen my comings and goings with the cart. He spread the word among the neighbors that the Glassmans' daughter was "bad." His imagination rendered me pregnant. He wrote my parents a note to that effect. My mother called and, weeping over the phone, asked me if this was true.

The crime of sex was like guilt by association—not visible to the eye of the outsider, but an act that could be rather easily conjectured. Consequences would make it manifest.

I, too, knew why I'd left—better than anyone. It was to be with Alex. He was the concrete embodiment of my more abstract desire to be "free." By which I meant—if I'd been pressed to admit it—sexually free. The desire for this kind of freedom subsumed every other. For this I was prepared to make my way in the world at the age of nineteen, incurring all the risks of waifdom on fifty dollars a week. In fact, fifty dollars seemed a lot to me, since I'd never had more than ten dollars in my pocket all at once. I opened a charge account at Lord and Taylor.

I didn't think I'd actually be living in my new room for very long. It was just until Alex and I got married. All I had to do was prove to him how different I was going to be, now I was no longer under my parents' roof. I would demonstrate how independent I was, how little I really expected from him. In my strange scheme of things, independence seemed the chief prerequisite for marriage. But it was for Alex's sake, not mine, that I was going to be independent.

In the room of my own, on the nights I was there—which became more and more frequent—I'd lie on my bed with my eyes wide open, waiting until it was time to go to sleep. I wouldn't feel homesick so much as uninhabited, like a coat Alex had taken off and hung up on a hook.

In the morning I'd inhabit myself again, getting up to go to the office, plunging into the subway rush hour. Emerging into daylight at Fiftieth Street, I'd feel I'd been swept into an enormous secretarial army advancing inexorably upon Madison Avenue. There was comfort in this, a way of leaving the girl on the bed behind me. As part of this army, I typed, read manuscripts, answered the phone, ate egg-salad sandwiches in the downstairs luncheonette (I'd learned very quickly to locate the cheapest item on a menu).

My boss, Naomi Burton, who'd hired me despite my lack of a B.A., took an interest in me. I was talented, she told me. I could become a literary agent myself if I worked for her for a few more years. She persuaded me to show her a story I'd written at Barnard and published in the college literary magazine. "You're a writer," she said. "You should try your hand at a novel." She rang up a friend of hers, an editor named Hiram Haydn who ran a famous novel workshop at the New School for Social Research, and asked him to let me into the course.

It was thrilling but terrifying—as if I were really in danger of fulfilling the destiny my mother had wanted for me, which I had gone to such lengths to avoid. It seemed to be happening to a person outside the person I really was. I'd hidden from my mother's eyes the story Naomi Burton was sending Hiram Haydn—a story I'd written over and over again in various forms ever since my high-school days—about a thirteen-year-old girl whose mother confides in her one day her bitter disappointment with her marriage.

Some time that year *Bonjour Tristesse* was published, causing a great furor in the United States. It was about a young French girl's loss of innocence in an affair with an older man married to a woman who had been very kind to her. The author, Françoise Sagan, was only a year older than I was. Her prose was like an elegant shrug of Gallic detachment and sophisticated regret. Sagan's schoolgirl face, knowing and slightly melancholy beneath her *gamin* haircut, appeared in every magazine and newspaper for a while. Her right thumb hovered just at the corner of her mouth, an indecisive gesture half infantile, half provocative. She seemed, however, to have taken possession of her fame with great aplomb, living it up the way young male writers were supposed to. She had a predilection for very fast driving in expensive sports cars; she dashed from literary parties to weekends at chateaux, alighting occasionally at cafés to be photographed with her thumb in its memorable position. Anyhow, that was my envious vision of her. She was a girl F. Scott Fitzgerald could have invented to torment poor Dick Diver. Americans forgave her amorality because she was French.

Sagan came to America for a few weeks, and Alex read every interview with her he could find. There was something in her speed, her coolness, that seemed to him totally new. He kept saying he wished there was some way he could meet her. Fortunately this wasn't likely. I loved Alex so much myself I was positive Sagan would find him irresistible.

Around April, Alex fell in love with a girl named Bobbie Weintraub, who wasn't anything like Sagan. He took her away from his roommate Anton, a graduate student in physics who'd moved in to share expenses and whom Bobbie visited on trumped-up overnight passes from the Barnard dorms. She was small and earnest and neat as a pin and planned to be a social worker; she'd always tidy up the living room on 112th Street much better than I could. She seemed either struck with wonder by everything Alex said or greatly shocked and offended by it, which he also enjoyed. One night she came over when Anton was at the library, and she and Alex went to bed. For weeks Anton threatened suicide.

I couldn't seem to get past my violent anguish. Each morning it would tear through me when I woke up remembering that Alex now wanted Bobbie Weintraub and not me. I knew that since I could never love anyone else, I was going to be alone for the rest of my life. "I want you as a friend," Alex insisted, but he'd only speak to me on the phone, always sounding curt and hurried and making it plain that if he met me anywhere, he'd have to bring Bobbie along as well.

"Try therapy," he'd urge me. "Promise me you'll try therapy."

In June I didn't get my period. First it was a little late, and then a lot, but I still thought it would come anyway, and I waited, thinking I felt it sometimes. But finally it didn't come. A tangible, unbelievable fact, like sealed doom.

I was going to have a baby. But it was impossible for me to have a baby.

The father wasn't Alex. The father was a child of my own age—a wrecked boy I'd known from Columbia who already had a drinking problem and lived, doing nothing, with his parents in Connecticut. I didn't love this boy. Sometimes you went to bed with people almost by mistake, at the end of late, shapeless nights when you'd stayed up so long it almost didn't matter—the thing was, not to go home. Such nights lacked premeditation, so you couldn't be very careful; you counted on a stranger's carefulness. The boy promised to pull out before the danger—but he didn't. And although I could have reminded him of his promise in time, I didn't do that either, remembering too late it was the middle of the month in a bedroom on East Ninety-sixth Street that smelled of smoke and soiled clothing, with leftover voices from that night's party outside the closed door.

I'd gotten a therapist by then—a $7.50 man, a rejected boyfriend of the woman whose apartment I was living in. I told him my problem. "I see," he said, rubbing his large chin, staring out over Central Park West.

There was a box of Kleenex on the small Danish-modern table near my head. He had pointedly placed boxes of tissues in several locations in his office. But I never cried.

I explained to this therapist why I didn't see how I could become a mother. Aside from being twenty years old, I lived on fifty dollars a week and had cut myself off from my family. I said I would rather die. And then I asked him what Elise had told me to: "Could you get me a therapeutic abortion?" (I'd never heard the term before she explained what it meant.)

"Oh, I wouldn't even try," he said.

I hadn't thought he wouldn't try.

Life was considered sacred. But independence could be punishable by death. The punishment for sex was, appropriately, sexual.

There were women in those days who kept slips of paper, like talismans to ward off disaster, on which were written the names of doctors who would perform illegal abortions. Neither Elise nor I knew any of these women. You had to ask around. You asked friends and they asked friends, and the ripples of asking people widened until some person whose face you might never see gave over the secret information that could save you. This could take time, and you only had two months, they said, and you'd lost one month anyway, through not being sure.

The therapist called my roommate, got from her the name of the boy who had made me pregnant. He called the boy and threatened to disclose the whole matter to his parents unless the boy came up with the money for an illegal abortion. The boy called me, drunk and wild with fear. I hadn't expected anything of this boy except one thing—that when I had an abortion he'd go there with me; there had to be someone with you, I felt, that you knew. But as for blaming this boy—I didn't. I knew I had somehow let this happen to me. There had been a moment in that bedroom on Ninety-sixth Street, a moment of blank suspension, of not caring whether I lived or died. It seemed important to continue to see this moment very clearly. I knew the boy wouldn't come with me now.

I went to see the therapist one last time to tell him he had done something terribly wrong.

"Yes," he admitted, looking sheepish. "I've probably made a mistake."

I said, "I'm never coming back. I owe you thirty-seven fifty. Try and get it."

Someone finally came up with a person who knew a certain doctor in Canarsie. If you called this person at the advertising agency where he worked, he wouldn't give you the doctor's name—he'd ask you if you wanted to have a drink with him in the Rainbow Room, and over martinis he might agree to escort you out to see the doctor. This person wasn't a great humanitarian; he was a young man who had a weird hobby—taking girls to get abortions. He'd ask you if you wanted to recuperate afterward at his house on Fire Island. You were advised to say no.

Blind dates were a popular social form of the fifties. As I sat in the cocktail lounge of the Rainbow Room, staring through the glass doors at crew-cutted young men in seersucker suits who came off the elevator lacking the red bow tie I'd been told to watch out for, I realized that despite the moment in the bedroom, I probably didn't want to die, since I seemed to be going to an enormous amount of effort to remain living. If it happened that I died after all, it would be an accident.

He turned up a half-hour late in his blue and white stripes. "Why, you're pretty," he said, pleased. He told me he liked blondes. He made a phone call after we had our drinks, and came back to the table to say the doctor would see us that night. "I hope you don't have anything lined up," he said.

He offered me sticks of Wrigley spearmint chewing gum on the BMT to Canarsie. People in jokes sometimes came from there, but I'd never been to that part of Brooklyn in my life.

Canarsie was rows of small brick houses with cement stoops and yards filled with wash and plaster saints. Boys were playing stickball in the dusk. You could disappear into Canarsie.

The doctor seemed angry that we had come, but he led us into his house after we rang the bell, and switched on a light in his waiting room. He was fat, with a lot of wiry grey hair on his forearms; a white shirt wet and rumpled with perspiration stretched over his belly. The room looked like a room in which only the very poor would ever wait. There were diplomas on the walls, framed behind dusty glass; I tried to read the Latin. He glared at me and said he wanted me to know he did tonsillectomies. To do "the other"—he didn't say *abortions*—disgusted him. I made efforts to nod politely.

My escort spoke up and said, "How about next week?"

"All right. Wednesday."

I felt panic at the thought of Wednesday. What if my mother called the office and found out I was sick, and came running over to the apartment? "No," I said, "Friday. It has to be Friday."

"Friday will cost you extra," the doctor said.

That night I called Alex and asked if he'd please go with me on the day of the abortion.

"Only if you and I and Bobbie can have a drink."

I'd managed to borrow the five hundred dollars from a friend in her late twenties, who'd borrowed it from a wealthy married man who was her lover. With the cash in a sealed envelope in my purse, I stood for an hour that Friday morning in front of a cigar store on Fourteenth Street, waiting for the young advertising executive. I got awfully scared that he wouldn't come. Could I find the doctor's house myself in those rows of nearly identical houses?

There was a haze over Fourteenth Street that made even the heat seem grey. I stared across the street at Klein's Department Store, where my mother had taken me shopping for bargains, and imagined myself dying a few hours later with the sign KLEIN's the last thing that flashed through my consciousness.

But finally the young man did materialize out of a cab. "Sorry to have kept you waiting." He'd brought some back issues of *The New Yorker*, and planned to catch up on his reading during the operation.

Upstairs in Canarsie, the doctor who did tonsillectomies had a room where he only did abortions. A freshly painted room where every surface was covered with white towels. He himself put on a mask and a white surgeon's gown. It was as if all that white was the color of his fear.

"Leave on the shoes!" he barked as I climbed up on his table almost fully clothed. Was I expected to make a run for it if the police rang his doorbell in the middle of the operation? He yelled at me to do this and do that, and it sent him into a rage that my legs were shaking, so how could he do what he had to do? But if I didn't want him to do it, that was all right with him. I said I wanted him to do it. I was crying. But he wouldn't take the money until after he'd given me the local anesthetic. He gave me one minute to change my mind before he handed me my purse.

The whole thing took two hours, but it seemed much longer through the pain. I had the impression that this doctor in all his fear was being extremely careful, that I was even lucky to have found him. He gave me pills when it was over, and told me I could call him only if anything went wrong. "But don't ever let me catch you back here again, young lady!"

I staggered down the cement steps of his house with my life. It was noon in Canarsie, an ordinary day in July. My escort was saying he thought it would be hard to find a cab, we should walk in the direction of the subway. On a street full of shops, I leaned against the window of a supermarket until he flagged one down. Color seemed to have come back into the world. Housewives passed in floral nylon dresses; diamonds of sunlight glinted off the windshields of cars.

On the cab ride across the Manhattan Bridge, the young man from the ad agency placed his hand on my shoulder. "I have this house out on Fire Island," he began. "I thought that this weekend—"

"No thanks," I said. "I'll be okay in the city."

He removed his hand, and asked if I'd drop him off at his office— "unless you mind going home alone."

I said I'd get there by myself.

KAY JOHNSON

Proximity

UNIVERSAL SPIRITUAL & PHYSICAL EXPRESSION OF LOVE POSSIBLE WITHOUT SIN, FORNICATION, OR ADULTERY . . .

So I have a game that I pretend, when I'm not allowed to pretend love, when no one else will pretend love with me. It's true I fall in love much more often than any one person is supposed to do. It's true that if I can be alone with any one person for an hour or two, I can achieve falling in love with him or her. But this is desperate, and they won't believe it, and they won't play it, my game of universal love. So I just go along, painting it.

For if they come again, I am all trembling.

For when I see them again, my eyes cry "Lover!" And they are all ashamed and embarrassed in front of me, for the husbands have wives and the wives have husbands already, and they do not understand this thing that I must do to them, having already done it to myself, for them.

They see me, and they run from me. They run because in that moment, their eyes acclaim me, in that moment my eyes gave myself to them, entered them, and in that moment, their eyes were opened . . . and their eyes cried, being open . . . and I painted this. Yea, and when I painted the husband, the wife bought the painting, saying it was for her alone. And when I painted the wife, the husband came wearing such a cold anger that I could not paint him at all.

And of those who are single, they are terrified.

For each wants to think that I speak only to him personally, and each wants to think that I want to possess him personally, and he only, and that the invitation in my eyes is for him personally, and not for everyone as much as it is for him. Each thinks that there is just *one* consummation of this love, that this love must bear its union in a physical, sexual consummation, and that if this cannot take place . . . the love was a lie, and it was not true. And they resent me for it and they run from me, because of it.

But what in the hell do people think Friendship *is*, if it is not love, if it is not the whole love, the complete love, the completely being in love, complete as with a lover. . . .

Yes, as proof of this thing, as proof of the reality of it, I could physically and mentally and emotionally sleep with every one of them, as Saint Francis kissed the leper, I could kiss each one of them, I could unite sexually with each one of them. But how can I stop with one? I cannot stop with one. I cannot even have one at a time. I want all of them. Everyone manages to stop with one. They get one lover, and they stop with one. You have no idea the amount of willpower this takes for them. They call it "infidelity," this overt expression of universal love, when it's expressed physically. But if souls love, the bodies are opened as easily, the bodies are only the houses the souls live in. If the soul is given, the body is open as easily. The soul is the key to it all, and where the soul is given, the body is open as easily.

And here's the trouble of it all.

They find if they let the soul flow out, the body is opened as easily, and everyone has no fidelity any longer, and everyone truly deep down in their soul, wants to love every one of them, as Saint Francis kissed the leper, I could everyone, and if we were all released from the barriers of our imaginations, the whole world would turn to an ecstatic holocaust . . . and we would all be throwing ourselves upon the bodies of each other constantly, indiscriminately.

Because this is the nature of us.

Only a few wild ones dare give in to it.

The rest of us play at it, play at it, I say, only.

These are called flirtations. We play at it, we joke, we kid each other about it.

Thus must the souls be damned, thus must the souls be damned up, lest they flow, for if they flow, then the bodies flow too, and have no power to stop themselves . . . thus would our souls and bodies go fornicating everywhere. . . .

Thus are people afraid of the love of the soul, thus must they damn their souls up separately within them, thus must they lock the soul in, thus must they deny it. . . .

For where the soul is completely given, where it is open, the body stands open as well . . . and to realize the potentiality for the essential whoredom of each of us . . . this is the monster that might threaten to undo us, this is the guilt that must be kept hidden. . . .

So heroically we inhibit, we pretend it is not so. And to achieve love on top of this denial of love, this takes a saint. But take our clothes off, and we are all saints in our most simple and passionate love for each other. . . . Remove our inhibitions, and the love of man for man and the love of man for woman and the love of woman for woman and the love of woman for man is all the most basic reality our souls and bodies have been created for . . . this touching of each other on our skins, the physical warmth of another body, this is what we were created for. Even the warmth of an animal, even a dog's lapping in our mouths with his solicitous tongue, there is pleasure there that he loves us and touches us, we could take pleasure in it, we could kiss the animal back, on his tongue, without tongue. Our tongues are willing, our hearts are willing, but something tells us this is wrong, this touching of wet tongues between two animals, this love, and so we have convinced ourselves it is repulsive, that we do not want to be got wet by his tongue, that it is an imposition of him to want to lap us up, and we will not surrender to it, no we will not surrender to any kind of love. And how we do succeed at this! Lordy. We succeed so that we draw away instinctively from a dog's wet tongue. We succeed to such an extent that we do not want his muddy paws on our clean clothes. We succeed to such an extent we have really convinced ourselves that our dresses, our white slacks, should not be over-run by dog hairs, by fleas, by animal smells, nor our skin even by his touch. . . .

We convince ourselves we don't like cats at all.

They, more than the dogs, are too openly sensuous. Do you know what they overtly do when they come and sit on your stomach at night? Do you know the rhythm they have, how with their paws they innocently knead your stomach and dare purr at the same time and rub themselves, their whole selves, against you, indecently as love and sensuality itself. . . .

Yea, should we give in to one, should we dare give into one, and love just one little animal, we should be undone for every dog and cat approaching us, we should be utterly undone for every human being approaching us. . . .

For the soul has been sublimated into sex.

Who did it, if Freud did not do it? Every yearning of the soul of man for man or the soul of woman for man or the soul of man for woman or of woman for woman, has been sublimated into a sexual significance, and this is all today that we are conscious of when we say love, when we say sensuality.

The dog, the cat, when they rub us with their flesh, yes, with their flesh, when the cat kneads and purrs, when the dogs want to kiss us in the mouths . . . oh the sensual and beautiful soul of the animal, it's not the full sexual union of its sexual organs with yours it's asking for . . . but simply closeness, the closeness of its little sensual soul, which IS its body . . . the touching of the skin . . . the lying down close to each other and curled up against each other . . . the transmitting of warmth from skin to skin, the transmitting of kisses and moisture . . . the lying close to each other for a long time . . . exchanging of something electrical, a charge that leaps from skin to skin . . . this touching of skins as friends lie down together, as friends want to be holding each other's hands, want to be putting an arm across a shoulder, want to be somehow unaccountably sitting close, next to each other.

This is in itself, fulfillment.

This is something which is not known, today.

This is something Freud had no idea of, that where there is love, there is no lust connected to the sexual organ, the lust is for looking, the lust is for proximity, the lust is for touching of the hand, the skin, the lust is for the interchange of some cosmic, electrical energy . . . and it is done, it is accomplished simply by proximity . . . by the sharing and exchanging of warmth, by the touching of skin to skin, it is done by body warmth, as a child, when it wants to be loved wants the body warmth of its mother, the skin contact.

The sexual organs have a different kind of love all by themselves. But the love simply of the skin for another skin, of one bodily warmth for another warmth, of the contact of one being for the contact of another being, this is a spiritual sensuosity . . . which does not *seek* to consummate itself, by the use of the sexual organs, which is satisfied innocently and fully and completely, simply by the sharing of warmth, by the skin contact, by the kiss, by moisture. . . .

And the soul is fully and innocently contented in this contact. *It* is contented, where there is the love of the soul. But where there is not the love of the soul, then the sexual organs rise and open in their own private lust, having nothing to do with the soul. Having private laws of their own.

And even where there is the love of the soul, all innocent and natural, society in its very fear of sexuality, *proclaims* that sex is what's wanted after all. So we aim for it, as if it were a target, and we will not be contented, no we will not *allow* ourselves to be contented, until we thrust our arrows in that red place, in the target's sexual centre.

But it is not sexual union the soul is after. It is some chemical interchange from skin to skin, from being to being, from proximity to proximity, from sitting next to each other, from sleeping in the same bed. From the clasping of hands, from the touching of skins.

poems from paris

. . . experience of 7 consecutive hours

Paris! My feet are cold and I feel better,
An hour in Paris with Verlaine,
In Greece another hour with Gregory Corso
On the Rue de Seine—
And it's home with a book of Zen—and two gold apples.
Paris, I love you again!
(My motion picture tape has happy pictures)

What if your flowers freeze in their stalls?
Your bargain apples closed behind 2:00 PM wire?
And the woman Soutine painted can never keep warm,
Wears Russian hat, boots, in Galerie des Jeunes
(I went in to paint, last week, but my feet got cold)

Affirmed or not affirmed, I'm the same one.
Spoken to, ignored, I am the same.
Loved or not loved, I am the same person.
And how's the battle going? Say, are you winning?
(I wanted poet-friends to confirm my being . . .)

Enough noumenal distress!—old river in me,
Rusty as the Seine, as old, as long;
Wrinkled with your old unjoyous burden,
River in me, what are you carrying?

What about this? Don't some people make me smaller?
But Corso says Greece is the color of tennis shoes.
Immediately my soul is greater than Greece.
(Poor old country, color of Corso's shoes!)
Immediately the world becomes my size.
My existence is profound: confirmed.

A bad picture of myself—i cringed two days
Got so small that i could hardly speak:
Dwindled, shrunken old head of myself, so dim.
How could i face the World? No Self-Respect.
Didn't i lose my battle for existence?
(How does it go today, Young Lover? Think you'll win?)
The psychic existence, is it really this precarious?
(One's feet in God—at least a place to stand,
A level for the mind to rest upon.)

Verlaine listening only to the bells.
He's one of the sounds of the city no one hears.
I can't hear any bells.
I take the metro; words come through the wheels:

"I am not fixed nor finished in perfection!
Delighted, I—These Universal Flaws!
So not unique, alone not miserable;
Mankind as I falls in my ravines. . . ."
And travel—doesn't it erase yourself?
Or your mistakes?
(Identity lost in God is Grand indeed!)

(now in French Class)
Suddenly what freedom—am I flying?
What release! What freedom from constriction!
From that small self—
But how ridiculous it is.
When I'm like that Everything frightens me!
(eating supper)
Just a small paranoia, not bigger than a cold;
(But whence the germs for the psychic chills?)

Oh Lord, to think how all activity
Inflated or had punctured me!
Imagine comedy of some New Mouse
(did i come to Paris just to see myself?)
Small as a Pebble growing High as a house!
But how ridiculous it is.
Larger and Smaller:
(a lifetime of this?)
Like long-necked Alice and her EAT ME pills!

Now shoulder to shoulder, tall as they,
(in the street)
I'm on the level with lovers, happy
I'm not ashamed looking into their faces.

. . . in Heaven at 9 Git-Le-Coeur

In Heaven they have rooms
very much like yours

—perhaps a little shabbier—
this one has 3 chairs and an ancient tile floor.

all the angels are complaining
because they don't get enough sun.
No one really minds, though.

Cats are not allowed.
There is only one fat cat, Miteau.
We have to take turns using it.
All the cats in Heaven are very fat.

People speak all languages,
though mostly French.
Doorknobs are in the middle of the doors.
People are all colors.

Everyone has a dream.
They talk from their souls.
Each goes around wrapped up in it.
They listen to yours.

No society.
Whom you like comes, whom you dislike goes away.
Not like or dislike.
Affinity.

Anything you want, talk.
Someone has one or is one.
Too much freedom makes you tired.
You have to sleep a lot.

One plays a flute all day and night.
Some rooms are classical, others bop.
The Housemother bawls everybody out
and makes them separate.

Angels congregate in clumps.
Sometimes these rooms are 20 angels thick.
Nobody objects to having no space.
They all like to touch.

The lights go on and off.
You use too much, a light flashes.
It rains on the roof.
The holes are covered by glass.

Voices in the walls
sound like little radios.
Alarm clocks every hour: from 6 AM
you can map this building.

In the Water Closets you have to stand up
on corrugated islands.
A Niagara rushes about your feet.
Funny, the feet never get wet.

Shoes never sit still.
Love is walking the floors day and night.
American voice crying, "Upstairs!"
Descending feet, a floor in flight.

It's cold in this room high up.
I can hear an angel cough.
They all have La Grippe now.
Writers give out rejection slips.

You can do whatever you want.
Nobody thinks you.
Nobody keeps appointments.
Nobody minds!

I can type here any hour.
I can paint without comment.
Everyone eats bread.
Reminds me: I have to have a tooth pulled.

But everyone in this Hotel lives.
Nobody ever dies.

HETTIE JONES

from How I Became Hettie Jones

The jazz that was the coming thing arrived that year at various downtown locations—Max Gordon's Vanguard on Sheridan Square in the heart of the old Village; the Half Note among the misty commercial streets of the Lower West Side; and on the East Side, the direction Roi and I took most often, in a bar reclaimed from the skids at the head of the Bowery on Cooper Square. For eighty years the Third Avenue El had blocked the sky there; now it was gone, leaving a space that looked surprised by its size, as if waiting for something new to fill it. The address of the small, low-ceilinged bar was 5 Cooper Square; the owners, two brothers named Termini, called it the Five Spot. In the summer of 1957 the composer-pianist Thelonious Monk was playing a long engagement. When you opened the door the music rushed out, like a flood of color onto the street.

Monk's chords explained to me, finally, why I'd always looked for the *wrong* notes on the piano. Every night I heard a new sound, or heard sound a new way. And I suddenly knew a score of new people—some of them Roi's friends from Newark—the trombonist Grachan Moncur, saxophonist Wayne Shorter and his trumpeter brother Allen, drummer Tom Perry, who read John Stuart Mill and died of drugs. There were so many more, a long list, including the master inventor Monk himself, carrying a furled umbrella, and then laughing at us when we gasped as he pulled out a sword! I remember a whole lot of laughter at the Five Spot. You can hear it on all the recordings made there. I think of us trying to laugh off the fifties, the pall of the Cold War, the nuclear fallout—right then, the papers were full of it—raining death on test sites in Nevada. I think we were trying to shake the time. Shake it off, shake it up, shake it down. A shakedown.

In the United States white people have historically made their way to places like the Five Spot in times like the late fifties—New Orleans, St. Louis, Chicago all had their scenes, whites went to the Harlem Renaissance, too. But it's important to the particular history of what would later be called the New Bohemia that going to the Five Spot was not like taking the A train to Harlem. Downtown was everyone's new place. The cafés were hosting new poetry, there were new abstract expressionist paintings in a row of storefront galleries on East

Tenth Street, new plays in new nook-and-cranny theaters—one of them, the Sullivan Street, in a basement up the block from the *Changer*. The jazz clubs were there among all of this. And all of us there—black and white—were strangers at first.

Black/white was still a slippery division to me. In Laurelton the rabbi had said Jews were a different people, but my schoolmate Mulligan's priest assured her that I was another race. The South had only served up reinforcement, and by 1957 I'd had little counterexperience. It would be two years before Philip Roth's Neil Klugman (in *Goodbye, Columbus*) described himself—with some difficulty—as "dark."

Music was my first written language—I read notes before words—and it had also come coded. In school, during World War II, we sang "I Am An American—Shout Wherever You May Be!" I knew America was the only place in the world where Jews weren't dead, but I didn't *feel* American; American was the Top 40s, and the Grand Ole Opry on the radio, the *goyische* Mozart and Chopin I played. It wasn't the Latin dance instructor who came with his records to our Laurelton basement—*Ola! La rhumba, cha cha cha, merengue!* And it most certainly wasn't those ancient, non-Western tones I loved to push through my nose: *Boruch atau adonai elohaynu melech haolum....* My family, who went to the synagogue once a year, called me *rebbitzen* (rabbi's wife). But I'd learned Hebrew only to sing it, and what I'd wanted to be—girls couldn't, until 1987—was a cantor, a *chazen*.

However, I entered the Five Spot, and all these other new doors I opened with Roi, as another image—one-half of the blackman/whitewoman couple, that stereotype of lady and stud. This was unsettling. Despite having been to school in the South—or maybe because of it—I was amazingly naïve about interracial sex. Separate bed, separate entrance, it was all the same to me. I didn't even have a full lexicon—I'd never come across the word *buck*, for instance. That summer *Dissent* magazine published Norman Mailer's essay "The White Negro." There I read that jazz was orgasm, which only blacks had figured out, and that white "hipsters" like me were attracted to the black world's sexy, existential violence. But the only violence I'd ever encountered, the one time I'd heard bone smashing bone, had been among whites in the South. The young black musicians I met didn't differ from other aspiring artists. And jazz music was complicated, technically the most interesting I'd heard, the hardest to play. All I wanted to do at the Five Spot was *listen*. Grachan Moncur told me I was the first white girl he'd ever met who came for the music and not for the kicks.

One night, after the last set was over, someone—not Monk

himself—began to play "Greensleeves" on the piano. He played tentatively at first, and then, as the harmonies settled, with chords that took the simple line into an elegant statement, a hymn. I guess he just took us to church, as people say, but this was more than the gospel I'd heard, or Mahalia Jackson at Newport, and I'd never felt this way outside a synagogue. A hush fell over the emptying club, and on either side of me spaces opened, and I could see the same feeling in all of us at once both apart and together, absorbing the clear, absolute notes.

From then on I never bothered with attitudes. It seemed as if another, new, language had been offered me, as old as the spirit I felt in myself, a music I could trust.

For those who still don't believe it, race disappears in the house—in the bathroom, under the covers, in the bedbugs in your common mattress, in the morning sleep in your eyes. It was a joke to us, that we were anything more than just the two of us together. We called the black/white lesbians next door "the interracial couple."

Still there's a certain kind of outdoor life when you're playing the other *Romeo and Juliet*, the one where nobody dies and hatred lurks, phantomlike, in every face except the most familiar, and can at any time become overt.

One moment stays in my mind. We were walking, early evening, along Bleecker Street, arm in arm. The catcalls began and continued. There weren't a half-dozen steady interracial couples in the Village. In 1950 thirty states still had miscegenation laws. I'd never even thought about that. When I understood that the jeers were for us, I turned. Ready to fight or preach, whatever my inexperience required. Nobody called *me* names.

But just as quickly Roi grabbed my arm again and pulled me around. Not violently, yet with an urgency I felt right away.

"Keep walking," he said. "Just keep on walking."

It was his tone that made me give in, and only later that I realized we might have been hurt, or *killed*—and him more likely—had we been out of New York City. My ignorance embarrassed me. The dangers became more obvious. Also, and most important, to live like this I would have to defer to his judgment.

This gave me some pause. I am not by nature obedient. I began to have moments when I felt we ought not to mess up each other's lives. I knew my family would be troublesome. Mostly I was haunted by the problem of remaining a Jew, but I didn't know how to reinvent a Jewish woman who wasn't a Jewish wife. "I think I am losing my Jewishness," I wrote in my journal, and then, "Grr . . . what is that?"

I looked up all my old boyfriends. I ran away one night with the motor-scooter man from Ferry Street. Roi wrote his first poem to me then, about how badly I'd treated him. I wept and was so contrite. Then he showed me a poem about "dancing" with another woman, one night while "his wife" was away. That was some relief, at least both of us were guilty.

But certainties always come down to me when I am not looking them up. Catching the sun one mid-September afternoon, I was sitting on the shallow step to the *Changer* with my knees drawn up under the wide skirt of my dress, and a copy of *Measure* magazine balanced on them. Roi always brought me books, or magazines of new writing such as this—Morton Street was littered with the latest and my head was full of it. All at once, intent on *Measure*, I took exception to something in a poem I was reading—about a man and a woman, written by a woman—and the very thought process, once begun, evoked such pleasure of illumination, such certainty about the opposite view I held—Well, *I'll* always be my *own* self is what I thought—that I leaned against the doorjamb, enraptured and full of the sun. Just then Roi came out, and slipped a hand over my head, and said, in his charming, word-playing way, "What's happening, McVappening?"

But when I turned to return the ball ("Whatdya mean, jelly bean?") I was still too enthralled with my vision to speak, so with one hand I held up the magazine, and with the other I pulled his fingers down to cover my face.

And then I grinned at him from behind his own hand.

And, at that moment, as he appeared to me in all his dapper, young, familiar self, all my last doubts disappeared. At the Five Spot the music had spoken, and now here were the words. The signs were clear. I would follow the language with this man, and find the tunes.

Soon after, at a party, I remet the critic's wife, the woman with whom I'd come home from Newport. She went on—and on!—about how different I seemed. I assured her that I was exactly the same, that only the season had changed, but I knew what she meant. There's nothing like love to make you look good. All the guests at the party had gathered in a circle, the host was Armenian, and we were doing a traditional Armenian dance. I was wearing my gray-green fedora with the peacock feather in the band, and new red Footsaver shoes. I probably had on long earrings, too. I was clapping and dancing and laughing and having a wonderful time.

"Now *she's* Armenian!" our host cried, pointing at me.

And Roi and I fell out laughing, in that way people would come to know and remember us, heads close, bodies leaning into one another, tight as ticks.

By then it had become so natural for us to be together that I didn't realize how obvious it was to others.

One Saturday, after a visit to Laurelton, my parents gave me a ride to the *Changer*. They were late and drove quickly away with only a wave at my welcomers.

Next visit my mother popped the question. "Who was that Negro boy?" she asked.

"My friend Roi," I said. "He works there too."

"Next thing you know you'll be living with him," she said.

I didn't answer. She was kneeling at the foot of the stairway, pinning a hem for me. I looked down at her round back, her mouth full of pins. I felt sorry that there'd be stress, as I knew there would be, about Roi. But I didn't feel compelled to discuss my affairs with my mother. I never had, and now I'd been away from home for nearly seven years, long enough, it's said, for all the cells of the body to change. My life with Roi was still a precious, new thing. I wasn't ready to give it away.

Not so my companion. One Sunday Roi woke up and decided he needed a haircut, and since his father was the family barber he called Newark and said we'd be over. An hour later, six blocks from my aunt's apartment, I stood, feeling near, far, shy, and hungry, on the Joneses' front porch. They had the first floor of a large frame two-family. The tree-lined street reminded me of Brooklyn.

It was Mr. Jones who answered the door. Slender as his son, he bent a gray head toward us paternally, and said, "Have some breakfast!" in one of those deep voices you normally find in a larger man, a very different tone from Roi's but full of the same confidence. He didn't seem in the least surprised to see me and neither did his wife, who was standing balanced back on her heels with her hands jammed in her skirt pockets. Her prematurely gray hair was exactly like her husband's; they were a matched pair, a set: he was a postman who was also a champion bowler—on the dining-room wall were shelves of trophies—and she was a social worker who'd been a runner (her own medals undisplayed, although she'd once been the second fastest woman in the world).

They'd just moved to this apartment, it was new to Roi. I realized as his parents showed us around that I'd been right to think of Brooklyn. The layout here was exactly that of the first home I remembered—the three steps to the cellar, the wide kitchen in back. All of a sudden I felt six years old.

While the haircut went on I helped Mrs. Jones make breakfast. She worked for the Newark Housing Authority. She'd been to Tuskegee and Fisk University. Roi resembled her. "How nice," she said, "that the two of you have similar interests."

He'd been right, I thought. His family *was* more middle-class than mine, better educated and worldlier. Actually, he could have patronized me.

"You know I wasn't here when Roi called, I was in a meeting at the Y," Mrs. Jones said. "But his father said he was bringing someone he wanted us to meet, so I came home." She smiled.

In a flood of relief I smiled back. She was telling me how much she loved her son. I knew she would understand—and appreciate—my own feelings for him. And I would tell her, when I knew her better, that I also liked to stand, like she did, with my hands in my pockets. My own mother had cautioned me against it—you'll stretch out your clothes, she'd said—but that was the stance, I thought, of a woman who stood her ground, a woman who'd take a stand.

Later that afternoon, Roi and I played softball with some of his high-school friends. I pitched, lefty me, and struck someone out. The pride on his face!

I thought about pride that night, back on Morton Street, with him asleep so peacefully close on the narrow bed. I was proud of him too—his quirky intelligence, his good humor, his stride. He was the first man I'd ever met who never failed to engage me. He was funny. He was even-tempered, easy, kind, responsible, and everyone else liked him too—I thought he was such a good *catch!* How I would have liked to show him off, to bring him out one Sunday on the railroad, to a Laurelton that might have shared my pleasure in him. But all I had to offer was this self of mine, in its alienation, behind me the burden of closed minds. There was a sad, dull fact to this, with ridiculous ironies. Because if I was the one who kept watermelon, it was Roi who loved a good sour pickle.

It's a sunny late September morning on Morton Street. We're hanging around, reading the paper. Roi's in a chair, one of the two the landlord said I might keep, and which, were we your typical fifties couple, we would now think of as "our furniture." Except we never think about furniture. Like money, it's simply what you come across. Luckily, we don't think much about food either—except the dollar salad at Café San Remo, split between the two of us, with lots of free bread and butter. (I haven't learned to cook.)

But we're living on love, of course. Last night we went to an Ionesco play, *The Bald Soprano*, and laughed louder than anyone else in the audience. That's another thing I like about us—we make noise. We play. He jumps over fire hydrants and tries to vault parking meters, eek. I whistle in the street, and tell him how my mother used to tell me to stop that. And when I am my usual antic self, the look of pleasure on him is like grace. With no effort, or adjustment, I can't imagine life without him.

And there's a way we approach the fact of our being together that has none of the high seriousness the world seems to wish on it. Little Rock, Arkansas, has just refused to integrate its schools. Federal troops were called. But nothing touches *us*; people stop and stare and we sail on—what else should we do, fall on our knees and ask their permission? Sometimes I still want to toss my head or stick out my tongue or shriek *We are not illegal* but I have learned, and I am learning every day.

Today I'm sprawled on the bed, thinking about what to do next. I've just finished reading the new, hot book *On the Road*. I love Jack Kerouac's footloose heroes, who've upset complacent America simply by driving through it! I don't know whether Roi and I are among "the mad ones, the ones who are mad to live, mad to talk, mad to be saved," but I know I don't want to go on the road right now, not while New York is the best place in the world. Nothing could tempt me away.

Though nagging my peace is the fact that Dick's dollar an hour is not enough anymore. Besides, he's running out of money himself and is thinking of closing the *Changer* and moving to California. I heave an elaborate sigh, a shoo-in for attention.

"What's the matter?" Roi comes up out of the *Book Review*.

"Hand me the want ads," I say gloomily.

He smiles at my terrible expression, but he'll be out of work soon too. "I'll read them," he offers.

I smile at him. How generous. But I don't hold much hope. I'll never find a job that's anything like the one at the *Record Changer*. It's probably back to the straight world for me. But where? What? And I don't *want* to. "Lots of luck," I say to Roi, and bury my face in the magazine.

Then in a few minutes he says, "Hey, look at this," and I hear disbelief. "Look at this," he says again. "*Partisan Review* wants a subscription manager."

"*Partisan Review*!" I jump off the bed. "Stop teasing me," I mutter, and crash down beside him, poking pages out of the way. "Let me see."

And, indeed, there it is. "Well, *I'm* a subscription manager," I say, incredulous. And then we're all over each other, laughing. But we remember to save the ad and the phone number.

The next day William Phillips, one of the editors, had nearly the same reaction. "You're really a subscription manager?" he asked. It must have seemed unlikely, not the kind of specialization expected from a drama major. But he was impressed by the fact that I'd done film research for Eric Barnaow at Columbia. (I didn't tell him I'd done that *once*.)

"And you *know* the magazine," he said doubtfully.

"Know *Partisan*? Why, of course," I said. "A friend of mine was discharged from the Air Force for reading it!"

This seemed to reassure William Phillips, who hired me on the spot. I left in a hazy euphoria. Eighty dollars a week and all those words! I couldn't imagine anything better, anything more thrilling—and the two, cluttered, scruffy rooms on Union Square confirmed all my rebellious suspicions. Here was real upward mobility—plus I got my job through the *New York Times*! What a joke!

Running downtown to spread the news, I caught my wide grin in Fifth Avenue's windows, above that same brown dress I'd worn home from Newport. And I'd been hired in my old clothes! Was it my direct eye, my innocent confidence? I'm curious now, I never thought of *why* then. The world was my oyster, that's all. And the pearls! . . .

Those two rooms were soon what the ads called a "one-girl office," since added to subscriptions were also "all phases magazine management." With literary quarterlies, international journals, *Dissent*, *Midstream*, *Hudson*, *Poetry*, *Kenyon*, *Encounter*, the London *Times*—and books, books! An ocean of words and opinion surrounded me like the jiffy bag fuzz I'd scatter each morning in my rush to open the mail.

And as Union Square was familiar, I preferred to hole up, noon hours, in the grimy-windowed *Partisan* office, with a peanut butter and jelly sandwich and whatever I happened to be reading.

In a very short time I discovered myself barely educated, with great intellectual gaps where everyone else had stored movements and cultures. What had I learned at Mary Washington—Roi called it my "teacup college"—except an illusion of independence from the men who called the shots? "That's the trouble with you young people today, no sense of history!" William would yell cheerfully, shaking his finger at me. Yet he was always kindly instructive, and I liked watching him edit, the care for the precise word, the very generosity of honing another person's argument. When I began to take charge of business with the printer, and there were times when a line here or there had to be saved, we would spread out the proofs and go over them. The content dissolved in the pleasure of sweet manipulation.

Still my mind balked at the academic focus on criticism, the same texts run over and over like obligatory laps. I imagined the nine letters of N.e.w. C.r.i.t.i.c. as the nine Supreme Court justices, presiding over all that was robed and respectable. And Moby-Dick, solid and impenetrable, with all these critics sliding down his sides. I knew William was right but sometimes I felt defensive, as if it were only *his* history he thought I should know. Where was the guide to my situation, cultural or political—where was my life in all these pages? I felt, as always, that I had no precedent. Except—to give credit where it's certainly due—the time William said to me, with a terrible look of astonishment: "What! You've never read Tillie Olsen!"

Fortunately, neither an acceptable *Moby-Dick* analysis, nor an enlightened Lenin approach, is much to the point in running a magazine, even a literary one, and with a sly acuity of eye and ear I could fudge it. The past regretted, I had no complaints about my present education. William's co-editor, the critic Philip Rahv, also seemed to trust me and like William was willing to teach.

"Copyedit this," he said to me one day, putting a manuscript into my hand.

"But I've never . . . how do you do it?" I said.

He hesitated, frowning, then patted my shoulder. "Just make it right," he said reassuringly. "And change it from English to American."

That I felt I could do. By luck I had grammar by ear, and knowing American was high on my list. What I didn't tell Philip, or William—not just yet—was that I thought we were defining American now, we of the "misalliance," we of the new world, the one that hadn't yet livened their pages.

The Mills Hotel, on Bleecker Street at Thompson, was a dank, cavernous, derelict's roost and occasional home to desperate artists. On the Thompson Street side it had a narrow café, which opened for a time as a coffeehouse called Jazz on the Wagon. Although the music was only occasional, and the place was funky and hastily constructed of plywood and the floor slanted, a small but provocative literary group sometimes gathered at the squeezed-up, wobbly tables. They even had a name— the "Beats"—ambiguous enough to include anyone.

Jack Kerouac had thought up "the Beat Generation," in conversation with another writer, John Clellon Holmes, who later explained *beat* as "pushed up against the wall of oneself." At the readings at the Wagon—and the Gaslight, Limelight, Figaro and other Village cafés— not all the poetry beat the agony. Roi and I were almost too sane in a group where shrink-time seemed mandatory. To be beat you needed a B-movie graininess, a saintly disaffection, a wild head of hair and a beard like the poet Tuli Kupferberg, or a look of provocative angst like Jack Micheline. Ted Joans was another beat picture, a black man always dressed in black, from a black beret on down. The women, like me, had all found Goldin Dance Supply on Eighth Street, where dirt-defying, indestructible tights could be bought—made only for dancers then and only in black—which freed you from fragile nylon stockings and the cold, unreliable, metal clips of a garter belt. The Beats *looked* okay to me, and I applauded their efforts, successful or not, to burst wide open—like the abstract expressionist painters had—the image of what could be (rightly) said.

Public readings were a new, qualitatively different route for writers. Few were in print and performance counted—how you sound, as Roi said. Besides Kerouac, the other beat hero-poet was Allen Ginsberg, whose *Howl And Other Poems*—published in San Francisco, in the fall of 1956, by Lawrence Ferlinghetti's City Lights Bookshop—had been seized by Customs and the police and tried for obscenity. (It won.) Roi got Allen's address in Paris and wrote him, on toilet paper, asking if he was "for real." Allen was pleased and responded. Roi was asked to read his own work. Soon we'd met the poets Gregory Corso, Diane Di Prima, and then Frank O'Hara, who was also a curator and took us to the Cedar Tavern to meet the Tenth Street painters—Larry Rivers and Alfred Leslie are the first of those I remember but soon I recognized more than a few and picked them out of the crowd at the Five Spot, where they also were regulars. At the Cedar we met many of the artists who'd studied and lived at Black Mountain College, the legendary home of avant-garde education, which had just closed. The days went by in a streak of events and performances. John Coltrane succeeded Monk as a main attraction. Atlantic Records advertised "the label in tune with the Beat Generation." In England a current play was described as a "soap opera of the Beat Generation, British version." One dark, jammed night at Jazz on the Wagon Roi and I were introduced to the suddenly famous Kerouac himself, a medium-sized, rather shy man. Critics had called him "a voice," but he seemed bewildered by the ardent young crowd for whom he'd spoken.

That fall, after the Russians sent up *Sputnik*, the world's first spacecraft, the suffix "nik" was added to beat, putting us square in the enemy camp. There was some humor—Ted Joans and photographer Fred McDarrah rented themselves to parties as "genuine beatniks," dressed appropriately and carrying a set of bongos, an instant symbol for Negro culture. Although like hipsters the Beats appreciated jazz, they weren't content to leave it where it had always been left—in its "place." Jack Kerouac's "spontaneous bop prosody," for instance, was an attempt to sophisticate the English language rhythmically, to make it *work*, like music. Like the writing of Martin Williams and Nat Hentoff, this did prefigure a different approach to black culture, and got on some literary nerves:

"Oh, man! man! man!" moaned Dean [in *On the Road*]. " . . . here we are at last going east together. . . . Sal, think of it, we'll dig Denver together and see what everybody's doing although that matters little to us, the point being that we know what IT is and we know TIME and we know that everything is really FINE. . . . Listen! Listen! . . . He was poking me furiously in the ribs to understand. I tried my wildest best. Bing, bang, it was all Yes! Yes! Yes! . . ."

It was only a ten-minute walk from the *Partisan* office to the Village hubbub. I brought what I'd learned, and judged Roi front line. Not just for love: I'd read enough to see that his voice was unique. He didn't use a lot of words, but then again he didn't have to. Sometimes, like Miles Davis says about notes, you just have to play the pretty ones. Roi wrote what he knew, from a fresh point of view. Onstage he was clear, musical, tough. He delivered.

He was also looking around for another job while finishing up at the *Changer*. Usually I met him there after work. One evening when I arrived he was on the phone. While he listened he kept gesturing at me and slapping his forehead. Then he said, "Yes, I'm well aware that he's a Negro, but he's been a fine employee. He hasn't stolen anything, if that's what you mean."

I gaped at him.

"We'd be glad to vouch," he said pleasantly, but with an expression that was new to me. His jaw muscles jumped, repeatedly and noticeably, as if he were gnashing his teeth while the rest of his face remained calm. It was a look I would come to know.

And this was the story: a record collector he'd seen about a job had just called the *Changer* to ask for a recommendation. Dick wasn't in. Thinking to get himself hired, Roi had pretended to be someone else.

Of course we laughed. But it brought home how suspect he was, simply being his competent self. Like, though so *un*like, most of our new friends. Yet often what was said about them applied to him most: "The freaks are fascinating," wrote one critic, "although they are hardly part of our lives."

My own life still worried me a little. Beside my desk at *Partisan* I kept a big green metal waste can, where most of my lunchtime attempts to write got filed. I was too ashamed to show them. I didn't like my tone of voice, the twist of my tongue. At the open readings, where anyone could stand up, I remained in the cheering audience. Roi was so much better; everyone else was so much better. Only one poem I wrote then survives, a sort-of-but-not-too haiku.

Nevertheless I didn't feel down for the count. All the Beats found it funny that I worked for the *Partisan* titans. Sometimes I hired Diane Di Prima, who had become a friend, to stuff envelopes and keep me company. I was able to bring Roi books and magazines. And at *Partisan* I could already see a stir of reaction, a gearing-up of the generations. William was considering poems by Allen Ginsberg and Gregory Corso. I felt happy to have landed—by remarkable, marvelous chance—in the middle.

But it was slick little Roi himself who made me feel most needed and wanted and appreciated, and it didn't seem (though this would change) that he loved me any less for my silence. But I did begin learning how to cook. My first pot of brown rice was inedible—a gummy off-tan mush. The two of us, hungry, stood peering into the pot in the little corner air-shaft kitchen on Morton Street. "What'd you do?" he said. "I don't know," I said. Still I felt nothing but hope in the future.

LENORE KANDEL

First They Slaughtered the Angels

I

First they slaughtered the angels
tying their thin white legs with wire cords
and
opening their silk throats with icy knives
They died fluttering their wings like chickens
and their immortal blood wet the burning earth

we watched from underground
from the gravestones, the crypts
chewing our bony fingers
and
shivering in our piss-stained winding sheets
The seraphs and the cherubim are gone
they have eaten them and cracked their bones for marrow
they have wiped their asses on angel feathers
and now they walk the rubbled streets with
eyes like fire pits

II

who finked on the angels?
who stole the holy grail and hocked it for a jug of wine?
who fucked up Gabriel's golden horn?
          was it an inside job?

who barbecued the lamb of god?
who flushed St. Peter's keys down the mouth of a
North Beach toilet?
who raped St. Mary with a plastic dildo stamped with the
Good Housekeeping seal of approval?
          was it an outside job?

where are our weapons?
where are our bludgeons, our flame throwers, our poison
gas, our hand grenades?
we fumble for our guns and our knees sprout credit cards,

we vomit canceled checks
standing spreadlegged with open sphincters weeping soap suds
from our radioactive eyes
and screaming
for the ultimate rifle
the messianic cannon
the paschal bomb

the bellies of women split open and children rip their
way out with bayonets
spitting blood in the eyes of blind midwives
before impaling themselves on their own swords

the penises of men are become blue steel machine guns,
they ejaculate bullets, they spread death as an orgasm

lovers roll in the bushes tearing at each other's genitals
with iron fingernails

fresh blood is served at health food bars in germ free
paper cups
gulped down by syphilitic club women
in papier-mâché masks
each one the same hand-painted face of Hamlet's mother
at the age of ten
we watch from underground
our eyes like periscopes
flinging our fingers to the dogs for candy bars
in an effort to still their barking
in an effort to keep the peace
in an effort to make friends and influence people

III

we have collapsed our collapsible bomb shelters
we have folded our folding life rafts
and at the count of twelve
they have all disintegrated into piles of rat shit
nourishing the growth of poison flowers
and venus pitcher plants

we huddle underground
hugging our porous chests with mildewed arms
listening to the slow blood drip from our severed veins

lifting the tops of our zippered skulls
to ventilate our brains
             they have murdered our angels

we have sold our bodies and our hours to the curious
we have paid off our childhood in dishwashers and milltowns
and rubbed salt upon our bleeding nerves
in the course of searching
             and they have shit upon the open mouth of god
they have hung the saints in straitjackets and they have
tranquilized the prophets
they have denied both christ and cock
and diagnosed buddha as catatonic
they have emasculated the priests and the holy men and
censored even the words of love
       Lobotomy for every man!
and they have nominated a eunuch for president
       Lobotomy for the housewife!
       Lobotomy for the business man!
       Lobotomy for the nursery schools!
and they have murdered the angels

IV

now in the alleyways the androgynes gather swinging their
lepers' bells like censers as they prepare the ritual
rape of god
       the grease that shines their lips is the fat of angels
       the blood that cakes their claws is the blood of angels

they are gathering in the streets and playing dice with
angel eyes
they are casting the last lots of armageddon

V

now in the aftermath of morning
we are rolling away the stones from underground, from the
caves
we have widened our peyote-visioned eyes
and rinsed our mouths with last night's wine
we have caulked the holes in our arms with dust and flung
libations at each other's feet

and we shall enter into the streets and walk among them and
do battle
holding our lean and empty hands upraised
we shall pass among the strangers of the world like a
bitter wind
and our blood will melt iron
and our breath will melt steel
we shall stare face to face with naked eyes
and our tears will make earthquakes
and our wailing will cause mountains to rise and the sun to
    halt

THEY SHALL MURDER NO MORE ANGELS!
            not even us

Love-Lust Poem

I want to fuck you
I want to fuck you all the parts and places
I want you all of me

all of me

my mouth is a wet pink cave
your tongue slides serpent in
stirring the inhabited depths
and then your body turns and
then your cock slides in my open mouth
velvety head against my soft pink lips
velvety head against my soft wet-velvet tongue
your cock /hard and strong/ grows stronger, throbs in my
    mouth
rubs against the wet slick walls, my fingers hold you
caress through the sweat damp hair
hold and caress your cock that slides in my mouth
I suck it in, all in, the sweet meat cock in my mouth and
your tongue slips wet and pointed and hot in my cunt
and my legs spread wide and wrap your head down into me

I am not sure where I leave off, where you begin
is there a difference, here in these soft permeable membranes?

you rise and lean over me
and plunge that spit-slick cock into my depth
your mouth is on mine
and the taste on your mouth is of me
and the taste on my mouth is of you

and moaning mouth into mouth

and moaning mouth into mouth

I want you to fuck me
I want you to fuck me all the parts and all the places
I want you all of me

all of me

I want this, I want our bodies sleek with sweat
whispering, biting, sucking
I want the goodness of it, the way it wraps around us
and pulls us incredibly together
I want to come and come and come
with your arms holding me tight against you
I want you to explode that hot spurt of pleasure inside me
and I want to lie there with you
smelling the good smell of fuck that's all over us
and you kiss me with that aching sweetness
and there is no end to love

Junk/Angel

I have seen the junkie angel winging his devious path over
        cities
his greenblack pinions parting the air with the sound of fog
I have seen him plummet to earth, folding
his feathered bat wings against his narrow flesh
pausing to share the orisons of some ecstatic acolyte
The bone shines through his face
and he exudes the rainbow odor of corruption
his eyes are spirals of green radioactive mist
luminous even in sunlight   even at noon
his footstep is precise, his glance is tender
he has no mouth nor any other feature
but whirling eyes above the glaring faceless face
he never speaks and always understands he answers no one
Radiant with a black green radiance
he extends his hollow fingered hands
blessing   blessing   blessing
his ichorous hollow fingers caressing the shadow of the man
with love and avarice
and Then unfurls his wings and rides the sky like an
enormous Christian bat   and voiceless
flies behind the sun

Blues for Sister Sally

I

moon-faced baby with cocaine arms
                nineteen summers
                nineteen lovers

   novice of the junkie angel
lay sister of mankind penitent
        sister in marijuana
        sister in hashish
        sister in morphine

against the bathroom grimy sink
pumping her arms full of life
                (holy holy)
she bears the stigma (holy holy) of the raving christ
                (holy holy)
        holy needle
        holy powder
        holy vein

dear miss lovelorn: my sister makes it with a hunk
of glass do you think this is normal miss lovelorn

I DEMAND AN ANSWER!

II

                weep
for my sister she walks with open veins
leaving her blood in the sewers of your cities
                from east coast
                to west coast
                to nowhere

   how shall we canonize our sister who is not quite dead
        who fornicates with strangers
        who masturbates with needles
who is afraid of the dark and wears her long hair soft and
        black
                against her bloodless face

III

midnight and the room dream-green and hazy
we are all part of the collage

> brother and sister, she leans against the wall
> and he, slipping the needle in her painless arm

> pale fingers (with love) against the pale arm

IV

children our afternoon is soft, we lean against each other

> our stash is in our elbows
> our fix is in our heads

god is a junkie and he has sold salvation
> for a week's supply

EILEEN KAUFMAN

from Who Wouldn't Walk with Tigers

Mark Green had been clueing me that there was really nothing going on in North Beach at the moment, but when Jack Kerouac, Allen Ginsberg, Bob Kaufman, and Neal Cassady came back, there really would be something happening.

The third week in May, Mark seemed unduly excited. He whispered to me, "That one there—in the red beret—that's Bob Kaufman."

I looked over. I saw a small, lithe brown man/boy in sandals . . . wearing a red corduroy jacket, some nondescript pants and striped t-shirt. A wine-colored beret was cocked at a precarious angle on a mop of black curly hair . . . and he was spouting poetry. A policeman came in and told Bob to cool it. He stopped—only until the cop left. Then once more, he began. This time, he jumped up on the nearest table in the Bagel Shop. "Hipsters, Flipsters and Finger-poppin' daddies, knock me your lobes." He was quoting one of his idols, Lord Buckley.

Next, he began to shout some of his own poetry. Everyone was laughing, listening to this poet. When he left the Bagel Shop, everyone within hearing seemed to leave with him. We all wandered over across the street to what was then Miss Smith's Tea Room. And Bob proceeded to hold court at a large round table like a latter-day François Villon.

Flashing black eyes dancing as he spoke, gesticulating as a European does. I couldn't believe this. It all seemed to me like a scene from one of my favorite operas that I had sung the year before.

Rodolfo from "La Bohème" must have appeared like this bard . . . even down to the black goatee. And watching Bob hold court in the Tea Room at the huge table filled with artist friends and admirers, generally leaving the bill for the enthralled tourist . . . it seemed very much that scene from Bohème wherein Musetta joins Marcello, Mimi, Rodolfo, and their artist friends, leaving her wealthy escort to pay their outrageous bill.

I think I began to play Mimi subconsciously—in the hope that this dynamic Rodolfo would notice me. No luck that evening, but a few nights later, still recuperating from my first head spinning peyote trip, instead of going off to Sacramento to write copy—I remained in the pad which my friend with the MGA and I maintained for weekends. We sublet it to Joe Overstreet, a painter, during the week.

There were four rooms with a long hall connecting them. One in back—a storeroom—a small kitchen, a bathroom, a tiny living room, and the bedroom which Joe used.

Lucky for me that I kept the apartment and used it. For it was on this night that Skippy, Bob Kaufman's old lady, chanced to throw him out.

I was still asleep beside Mark Green when I heard the voice I recognized from the Bagel Shop.

"Let me in. I need a cuppa' coffee . . . you know?"

That voice was hoarse and low. If you ever heard it, you could never mistake it for another. After ten minutes of Bob's pleading, Joe Overstreet came in and said, "For God's sake, somebody, get Bob Kaufman a cup of coffee so we can all get some sleep."

I got up, curious to see the small brown bard again. I went to the window. Mark was visibly annoyed. I padded over and opened the door. "Just a minute, o.k.?"

Suddenly I was looking into the deepest brown eyes I have ever seen—a well I was to explore for many years. I asked him in. Bob never stopped his monologue.

"Hey, man . . . my old lady, she threw me out . . . and I need a cuppa' coffee . . . Can you give me a cup, huh? I don't even have a dime . . ." and on . . . and on, while I slipped on my poncho over black leotards and t-shirt.

We walked down Kearny, crossing Broadway, over to the original old Hot Dog Palace on Columbus, where El Cid now sprawls on the triangle. Bob sat on a stool near the door. It was such a tiny place that anywhere you sat, it was near the door.

I paid for three cups of coffee for Bob while I drank hot chocolate. All the time we were there, he was charming everyone within earshot with his poetry, his quotations of great poetry of the ages, and his extraordinary insights. I was so completely overwhelmed by this young poet that I lost all sense of time, forgot my surroundings . . . everything banal.

Bob was teaching. Money was not important . . . a fact that I was fast coming to believe . . . Living was. Awareness is all. High on Life.

Time drifted by in the Hot Dog Palace. Bob was rapping on every subject known to Man . . . giving us all a show . . . expounding on history, literature, politics, painting, music . . . He kept repeating after every heavy subject that his old lady had thrown him out . . . truly confused that such a thing could be.

We finally left the stand. We walked in the damp San Francisco fog up the Kearny Steps. It might have been the Steppes of Central Asia. It might have been Hawaii. I was neither hot nor cold. I could only hear that hoarse, low voice.

When we got to the flat, I asked Mark for the key to his apartment on Telegraph Hill. I didn't want to disturb Joe further. We three walked to Mark's pad below Coit Tower.

Bob kept up a running conversation, and Mark went to the kitchen to look for food and tea. We just couldn't talk to each other enough. There were so many things we had to find out about each other all at once. Bob had seen a poem of mine which Mark had pinned on the Bagel Shop wall, without my knowledge.

Then Bob quoted one of his own poems to me. "An African Dream."

> In black core of Night, it explodes
> Silvery thunder, rolling back my brain,
> Bursting copper screens, memory worlds
> Deep in star-fed beds of time,
> Seducing my soul to diamond fires of night.
> Faint outline, a ship—momentary fright,
> Lifted on waves of color,
> Sunk in pits of light,
> Drummed back through time,
> Hummed back though mind,
> Drumming, cracking the night,
> Strange forest songs, skin sounds
> Crashing through—no longer strange,
> Incestuous yellow flowers tearing
> Magic from the earth,
> Moon-dipped rituals, led
> By a scarlet god.
> Caressed by ebony maidens
> With daylight eyes,
> Purple garments,
> Noses that twitch,
> Singing young girl songs
> Of an ancient love
> In dark, sunless places
> Where memories are sealed,
> Burned in eyes of tigers.

Suddenly wise, I fight the dream.
Green screams enfold my night.

I was overwhelmed. Here was a real poet. He reminded me of Coleridge, my childhood favorite. Bob was not one of those schlock artists who write just to be doing something. This man was real, a genuine poet with that calling.

I thrilled every time I looked into his dark, serious eyes. It wasn't hypnotism, because I was fully conscious. But the dynamic glance and depth of this poet's eyes was too much to bear for seven hours. This is how long we talked. We had to get through to each other immediately. I knew that I had suddenly fallen in love with a poet. I had been entranced—from the moment Bob began to talk . . . running down the hill, hand in hand, to the Hot Dog Palace.

We left Mark at his pad (I can't really say that I considered his feelings. I was too mad about Bob Kaufman). My Rodolfo and I wandered back to my flat hand in hand. Joe slept on—unaware of the changes I was experiencing. We sat down on a mattress in the back room and talked softly.

"You are my woman, you know," said Bob. I just gazed at him with newly opened eyes, now wide in disbelief.

He whispered, "You don't believe me now . . . but you'll see."

His arm was around my shoulders. I was standing next to him. I swayed a little then, and he caught me in his arms, broke my balance, and together—we fell laughing onto the bare mattress. He was laughing at me, and I was laughing because, well, I was a little scared and kind of high from our meeting and subsequent conversation.

Suddenly, I sat up straight and leaned over Bob, letting my hair fall into his face. He took hold of my long, loose hair with one hand and pulled me down to him. Then he kissed me. Except for holding hands or casually putting his arm about my shoulders, that was the first actual physical contact with him.

I shivered, and he pulled my hair a little harder, and consequently me closer. How did I feel? Like sunsets and dawns and balmy midnights and ocean voyages. My pulse was dancing a wild Gypsy rhythm, and I felt alive! We searched each other's mouths for a time. Then, as if we had found an answer there . . . without a word, we broke apart . . . and each began to undress the other.

It was a simple task for me, because Bob wore only trousers, t-shirt and sandals. I was eager to feel his strong brown body. It seemed a long time until I was in his arms and stroking that sensual body. This man—with the body of Michelangelo's David—wanted me—and yes, oh yes, I certainly wanted him—for as long as he would have me.

When you find your soul mate, there can be no question, no hesitation, no games. You have been lovers before in many other lives, so you are attuned to each other immediately.

Why else is there love at first sight? Hollywood is often chided for its use of music coming out of nowhere in a big love scene. Believe me, there is music then—music from the spheres.

Without the slightest formal introduction on my part to Eastern eroticism, Bob and I became Tantric lovers spontaneously that morning. That was my second psychedelic trip in two weeks in North Beach.

It is true that your soul leaves your body during a very passionate love embrace. It happened to me just that way. And I suspect that Bob experienced a bit of magic too . . . as he held me throughout the entire tidal wave.

When I caught my breath, I looked at him and smiled. I noticed that he was lying beside me drenched and spent. He said it again. "You see? You are my woman. You have absolutely no choice in the matter."

For the first time, I began to think. How can you ponder what is happening in a vortex . . . at the eye of the hurricane . . . in a whirlpool? You can only swing with it and hope you don't go under permanently. Was I going under? Up to this point, I hadn't even cared.

But now, I leaned on one elbow and looked down into Bob's smiling eyes. I said it as well as I could. "It's just all too overwhelming for me, Bob Kaufman. Go away please and leave me for a few hours . . . till maybe 6 tonight, o.k? I really have to think about everything that's happened last night and this morning."

Bob's smile faded.

"But hold me now. We can talk later," I added.

He brightened and seemed to understand. He turned on his side, folded me back into his arms, and went to sleep. I may have slept, but I heard him when he got up to dress. I opened my eyes and said sleepily . . . "See you around 6 tonight . . . on Grant."

Bob said, "Then you'll be my old lady. You have no . . ."

I put my fingers over his mouth lightly. "Tell you then. I really have to be alone all day to think it out. Bye."

Bob kissed me lightly on the mouth and vanished. He was gone as suddenly as he had arrived.

I danced the rest of the day through in a hazy kind of mist. I wasn't high on peyote any longer. I was high on Bob Kaufman. Maybe contact high—maybe more, since he had all kinds of dope available to him . . . and he has never been known to turn down any of it!

I dressed slowly, brushing my hair overtime, taking a little more care with the black eyeliner . . . too excited to eat anything, I threw on my poncho and ran out the front door. We didn't have a clock in the pad, and I wasn't going to be late for this important decision.

I ran down Green Street, turned the corner at Grant. Walking down past the Bagel Shop, I saw Bob on the opposite side of the street. He stared at me intently and clenched his teeth, as he has a way of doing when asking a silent question. I just nodded. He came bounding across the street. I said, "You're right. *I'm your woman*." And he hugged me tightly in answer.

We started to the Bagel Shop. Bob read a few victory poems there, drank a few beers and laughed a lot. He told everyone, "Meet Eileen, my old lady."

That very night, I got my first taste of life with a poet. And that taste has since stayed in my mouth. I could never love a lesser man than an artist.

Bob began to hold court in the Coffee Gallery about 7:30 in the evenings, and for several hours while the locals and the tourists brought him beer, wine, champagne—anything, he, in turn, would speak spontaneously on any subject, quote great poetry by Lorca, T. S. Eliot, e e cummings, or himself. I would just sit adoringly at his side.

I wish that I had been able to tape every conversation, every fragment, because each time Bob speaks it is a gem in a crown of oratory. His wit . . . Cities should be built on one side of the Street . . . His one-liners . . . Laughter sounds orange at Night . . . and his prophecies—all are astounding. Bob's entire monologue is like a long vine of poetry which continually erupts into flowers.

In the late '50s the Coffee Gallery was arranged differently. After the management took over from Miss Smith, the Gallery became the "other" place in the 1300 block on Grant.

There was no partition for the entertainment section, and jazz was played throughout the place any time the musicians fell by. Spontaneity was the key word in our life style in North Beach. This is what made it "the scene," for one never knew in advance just who might show to read a poem, dance, play some jazz, or put on a complete play.

The tourists were delighted to buy a pitcher of beer, bottle of champagne, or anything we wanted—just to be a part of the life emanating from our table. The Life was, for the most part, Bob, and his hilarious monologues, sparkling wit and funky comments. Even the

"Mr. Jones" who didn't know what was happening in the late '50s knew that *something* groovy was going on, and he would *buy* his way into it, by God, if he couldn't get in any other way! That's where we accumulated our camp followers, hangers-on and groupies.

Some nights Bob would really get it on. In the early evening he would be writing on note paper, napkins, finally toilet paper, just to get his speeding thoughts down. I began to keep these valuable fragments for him so that he could finish the poems when he got home.

In the early morning, Bob would wander out and take one of his dawn-morning walks—harking back to walks with his great-grand-mother. Sometimes I would go with him. Other days I would sleep in. Bob and I would begin our Grant Avenue odyssey around three or four each afternoon. And whatever happened would happen. We would run down the hill, laughing, and brighten the lives of tourists, adding to the disorder of the day. We proceeded to urge on any musical activity in Washington Square. (New Yorkers, please note: We have our own in North Beach.) Bob might recite a poem or write a new one in the Bagel Shop . . . or we might drink wine or smoke grass at someone's subterranean pad. We spent a lot of time on the rooftops smoking hash.

When I met Bob Kaufman, King of North Beach, my values changed overnight. I had been a greedy, mercenary career girl whose only object was to get it while you can. But the very night I met Bob, I could see these values totally changing. When Bob read "African Dream" to me, I knew I had met a genius.

And so I knew at once what my life would be: Tempestuous, Adventurous, Passionate, but always new experiences. I reached out for Bob Kaufman, the man and his poetry. And he made my life a shambles. It was not as though I didn't ask for it. I knew at a glance and after one night that this man could create my life or destroy it. The life I had known was in ashes, and like the Phoenix, my new life had begun. It was to be everything I had seen in the flash of an African Dream . . . and more. Suddenly wise, I did not fight the Dream.

FRANKIE "EDIE" KEROUAC-PARKER

from You'll Be Okay

Following the abortion of our child, Jack Kerouac and I decided to get our own apartment. We would drop out of school and work, so that Jack could keep writing. We started looking immediately with a friend of mine, a Barnard student who was married to an infantry soldier. Her name was Joan Vollmer Adams. We found the right place at 420 West 119th Street, Apartment #28, in the New Year of 1942, just after the attack of Pearl Harbor.

Joan's husband, Paul Adams, was a Columbia law student, serving in the Army. She got his allotment checks, plus a good healthy allowance for attendance at Barnard. I also received an allowance from my family in Detroit, and I would be attending Columbia in the spring as a special student, to study painting with George Grosz. We used Joan's name, as a respectable married lady, to apply for the lease.

We were all going home for Easter, and coming back for summer school, so it was just as well we didn't have to plunk down the money until spring. The war was bulging Columbia with 90 day wonders in the naval officer program, and good apartments were not easy to come by.

Joan, Jack, and I went back to our separate parts of the U.S., most of us by train. I got the Empire State at 7:00 am out of Grand Central Station, standing all the way home, since, as the war went on, there were no reserved seats. I arrived in Detroit about 10:30 pm the same night. The train cost about $23.00; the cab ride home to Grosse Pointe from the Michigan Central Station (9 miles) was $3.00! I lived downstairs, in a two-family flat in Grosse Pointe Park, with my mother and younger sister, both named Charlotte Frances (Jack called my sister Francis in *The Town and the City*). My mother owned and operated Ground Gripper Shoes, in downtown Detroit, working six days per week, eight hours per day. My sister was in high school and had her special gang, as I did mine. People in Grosse Pointe were not lacking anything in those days except enough things to spend money on!

My gang was very close knit, so special that we even had our own language (we called it "turkey talk"). It was spoken by very few, and never understood by outsiders. It came in handy in school, with teachers never catching on. I never read books for pleasure, and I rarely cracked a school book! I was thrilled at the new world Jack was opening up to me.

When I returned to New York, after the Easter recess, there was a message from Albany to call Joan. She told me that she had this apartment, right around the corner from my grandmother's apartment, that she had leased it in her name and Mr. and Mrs. John Kerouac. Everything was working. I couldn't believe it; all our plans were falling into place. I asked if she had written Jack, and she said, "No." So I thought what a surprise I would have for him! Then Joan said it was only partially furnished. What fun we would have fixing it up! I hung up, and went upstairs to bed. Later, I used the janitor's phone in the back foyer, behind the elevator, when Jack called me, because my deaf grandmother did not have a phone in her apartment.

The next morning, after taking Rex, my grandmother's dog, for his walk, I raced over to 119th Street. It was a very "swanky" building, even had a little grass in the front. It was between Amsterdam and Morningside on the right side, #420, near the Kingsley Arms. It had a switchboard, with an operator, who gave me the key. It had an open gilt cage elevator with an attendant who took me up to our floor. What class! It was four stories up. I opened the door and pranced in!

It had two bedrooms, a good sized kitchen, a big living room, and it looked out on a courtyard. It was bright and cheery. There were four huge windows overlooking this courtyard, and a fire escape that went all across, which you could sit on to get the sunshine. All the surrounding apartments were occupied by Juilliard students—sopranos were singing constantly, along with their canaries!—they all had birds. It was like being on a "Broadway stage" with the cast and all included for $44.00 per month! I was really excited—my first apartment, on my own, and with my LOVE, JACK, my whole being was singing, along with a soprano giving her all, in the courtyard.

In the late afternoon, I met Jack at the Lion's Den. He had a cigarette dangling from his lips and was leaning in the doorway, very suave, with a heavy red and black wool check shirt and dark pants. He casually hugged me with one arm. He smelled good, like Lowell, and oh! so handsome! He picked up his suitcase, and we walked across Broadway, into the West End Bar, into OUR booth. He sat me down, and got us two beers. He sat across from me and we held hands across the table. I told him about the apartment. My God. Could there ever be a more wonderful day than this?

The war was upon us. We felt as if we had very little time. We had to be alone, our love was choking us; we needed each other, desperately. So off we went to our new apartment, and I was almost a new "pretend" bride, for we were Mr. and Mrs. here, and they addressed us as such. I can't recall if there was a bed. I know we owned a mattress and had plenty of candles! Comfort was not on our minds. Later we got a bed that was all iron, three quarter size and spring-like extension that came out from underneath to make it into a double bed; it was horrible! but we were in heaven! I had spending money, and then some, in the Corn Exchange Bank at 110th Street and Broadway.

We were all meeting at the West End Bar on Broadway and 114th Street for dinner and beer. Our conversations were stimulating, about the war creeping into our lives, plus all the new and exciting things at school, and New York City. We could never get it all said, nor begin to get it all done, but we tried, and there was Jack—writing it all down!

Columbia University at this time was an all men's school. The fraternity houses were all closed because of "Communist influence," of the past few years, so if you wanted to meet, the West End *was the place*. Suddenly, I had a lot of women acquaintances, who drifted in and out of our lives, but Joan and I were the mainstays of our group.

Jack, Joan, and I had to get down to business, getting jobs to support our apartment. So we started to think about the easiest way for the most money! Jack had to get the closest job that involved the least amount of time, for Joan and I agreed that his time was to be spent on "writing"—that was most important. So Jack went across the street and got a job at Columbia as a waiter. That way, he could bring food back to #28! Joan and I focused on the want ads.

Joan got a job addressing envelopes, typing, and Jack helped her in this department. Joan also corrected students' papers for spelling and punctuation, typing them neatly. She was a very brilliant woman. I am much more physical, also mechanical, perhaps as a result of growing up in the Motor City! I could drive anything. So I got a job as a "longshoreman!" Jack saw the notice on the board in his Merchant Marine Union Hall, because all the longshoremen were shipping out. There was no one with "operator's license" to take over their important jobs of loading the ships. I started working a 10 hour shift at the New York Port of Embarcation, located at First Avenue and 59th Street in Brooklyn, an Army base at that time. I made 85 cents per hour, probably equal to $8.00 now. I drove a forklift, tow motors and Clarks, large and small. When you drive these vehicles, usually loaded with pallettes, you alway drive backwards! To this day, I can drive better backwards than forward! Then I would drive an electric, four wheel cart, with six trailers, loaded: Rosie the Riveter indeed! I would take them down the pier, backing up the last trailer, so that the winch could pick up each pallette, up to "load" capacity. I loved this job, but 12 hour days (an hour each way on the subway) were exhausting. I was popping vitamins and eating like a longshoreman! During the winter, I wore eight sweaters, plus sailor, navy wool pants, and a pea jacket. Women only wore slacks in the movies at that time, so you couldn't buy them. When I worked, I looked like an overstuffed wrestler! but it was "damn" cold near the ocean.

Jack and I became friends with my boss, a very kind, sharp Black man, Roderick C. Bacote. He often came to the apartment for drinks and to talk about Jack shipping out. Secretly, of course, I hoped it would be a long time before he would have to leave me. Ronnie was always trying to give me easier jobs, and one was working in the warehouse, loading elevators, or storing. The hardest job to handle was coffee and sugar, for these were in bags and were easily spilled! But I loved this too; it was a challenge.

One morning on the 7:00 am shift, everything changed. I found an Army guard in the warehouse who had shot his brains out, at the shipping point. I had to go home that day—Jack was shook up too; it brought a new aspect of the war into our lives. From then on, I tried to avoid the warehouse. When working at night, we would finish loading the Liberty ships, then watch the soldiers board, then watch them pull out, go down the Hudson, and perhaps "way off," see a glow on the horizon, hoping it wasn't our ship being torpedoed—knowing the German "U" Boats were out there; the "Wolf Pack" even surfaced along the shore at night. What an experience the war was, even here in the U.S.

When he could, Jack went to the Union Hall looking for a ship. His habit was to write all night long, waking me up about dawn. I would make him a gigantic breakfast, milk instead of coffee. Rarely did he discuss what he wrote with me. As a matter of fact, early in the morning was a quiet time for him; he would be on his way to bed and sometimes I would go with him, depending on when I worked, and the weather! He had high body heat. He slept on his stomach with one arm in the air, or above his head, so the three-quarter bed wasn't enough for the two of us to "spreadoutsky!"

Jack would wake up around noon and go to his job, or the Union Hall, or read at home, or go to the Columbia library. He would leave me notes; none of us were people to call or talk on the phone. I am still the same way, but Jack's later years reversed this habit: he developed "diarrhea of the mouth!" on long distance. His family was in Lowell, and they would write him frequently; his mother almost every day. Jack would answer once a week. He wasn't big on letter writing.

Finally, the dreaded day came. As was his fashion, Jack never said a word. He would be especially sweet and talkative, and would try to have me not go to work. He would have the entire next day all planned—sleep in late after a wonderful night of "love making," and take a bath together. Our bathroom was his private domain, and to allow me in there was really something! Then we would go to a special place for lunch, Jack Delaney's on Sheridan Square in the Village, followed by walking around the art galleries up to the Museum of Modern Art for tea and dessert on the patio! I asked him what was on his mind? Nothing!

We got on the Riverside double-decker bus, sat upstairs, and headed uptown towards Columbia. We got off at 96th Street and walked, holding hands, up to Broadway where we went into Barton's Chocolates. We bought a two pound box of truffles. Jack adored these. Then we slowly started up Broadway, went into a pet shop (one of my favorite things to do), looked, petted, and cooed! All of a sudden Jack said: "Isn't that little black puppy cute?" "Yes!" I agreed. "It's a cocker spaniel." So Jack took it out of the cage, and put it in my arms. It was four months old, and weighed twelve pounds. The price was $6.00. "Why so little?" "No papers, last litter, just a female!" Jack said: "We'll take it," and handed the clerk $6.00. I was dumbfounded. Jack's impulses were rare. We got a rope for the dog and started to walk home. We were broke then. That darling little thing couldn't walk very far so we took turns carrying her, and named her "Woof-It!" Then Jack finally told me he had a ship, and would be leaving soon for Lowell, then Boston, then to board the S. S. *George Weems* to who knows where? So that was the reason for the puppy, to keep me busy, so I wouldn't be lonely. What could I do? Be grateful for the last night, today, and the puppy.

Let me tell you about Joan, because she was to become the closest friend to Jack and me, and the dearest girl I have ever known. Her influence is still with me.

Joan Vollmer Adams was her full handle through all her years of tears. She was from a suburb of Albany in upstate New York. Her parents were not divorced (mine were), and she had one, very nice

rother. Joan adored her father and disliked her mother. Joan
y's figure, with nice boobs, thick legs like an athlete—which she
—and when she walked, her calves wiggled! She was the most
fe.. .ine girl I ever knew. She wore some makeup, eyeshadow, powder
and lipstick.

Joan did not do things in a hurry—either walking, speaking,
dressing, or cooking. She read SLOWLY, as if she was savoring every
moment. She was taller than I, five feet, six inches; she had a beautiful
face, shaped a little like a heart, with small squarish jaw, thin lips, small
upturned nose, eyes wide apart, brown eyes that were large and soft.
Her hair was straight, light brown, thin, and she wore short bangs, had
her hair curled slightly on the ends, shoulder length. She always wore
bandannas, tied attractively up and tight to her head, always subdued in
colors. She was what you would call soft and dewy. The only thing
lacking was a Southern drawl. Now Joan's mind was another thing! She
was the most intelligent woman I have ever known. Joan was a reading
addict. Jack called her a "newspaper Neurotic," for every day she would
read, from stem to stern, every newspaper in New York City: *P. M.*,
*Daily Worker, New York Times, New York Herald, New York Post, Daily
News*, and anything else she could find. What was so amazing, she did
this in the bathtub, with warm bubbled, perfumed water, right up to her
chin! If you wanted to talk to her, anybody and everybody, you had to
do it in the bathroom. She had a gorgeous complexion, and always a
teensy tan.

Joan remembered everything she read and could speak on all
subjects, mostly on the writers we were all reading. Proust was her
favorite. She loved classical music, but also "Danny Boy." She hummed
this under her breath. Her idea of a good time was to sip Kummel
liqueur at Child's on Broadway and have intellectual conversations and
soft, sad music.

Joan always wore soft silk stockings (nylons were just showing
up, and panty hose were never heard of at that time), medium pumps,
and silky, clinging, feminine clothes that could cling to her attractive,
square body. She reminded us all of Greta Garbo. I was exactly the
opposite!

After two years in our 119th Street "station," Joan got a telegram one
Sunday morning, telling her that Paul was visiting on Medical Leave.
He was a law student at Columbia, but had been stationed in Tennessee.
I remember because he had fungus on his feet from swamp training. I

had never met Joan's husband, and I was a little nervous. I arranged to stay in my old room with my grandmother, and came back to #28 to feed and run Woof-It.

Jack was then in Norfolk, Virgina, near Washington D.C., in boot camp. I received a postcard; he hated it, he hoped to become a gunner, since they did not put him in Air Force School. Jack was on his way out of the "cuckoo" service!

I was still a longshoreman at the New York Port. Grandmother wrote to my mother in Grosse Pointe that I went to work looking like a plumber. I was wearing Henri Cru's pea coat and Navy bellbottoms, with all those buttons. I wore khaki pants in summer.

I went over to #28, two blocks away, to walk Woof-It, and Paul was there. Joan was excited when she introduced us. We had coffee.

Paul was very handsome, had light brown hair, eyes that matched, and huge shoulders. When we got up from the kitchen table, I saw that he was well over six foot tall. He spoke very softly, and he did not have an accent. Nor did Joan; I have a Midwestern twang.

Paul liked to read. Most of his books in our apartment had an inscription on the first page, "Semper Lumen," a Latin term Joan said meant "forever lighted." Paul was out of uniform lounging, so I didn't stay too long. His furlough was just two weeks. He was having his feet treated at Fort Dix, Long Branch, New Jersey.

Walking up Amsterdam Avenue, it had all turned green and warm, and the daffodils were just opening and the scent floated up to me from Columbia President Nicholas Murray Butler's garden. This lovely garden was right on the corner of 116th and Amsterdam. You could look right into it from my grandmother's apartment and see all the flowers and the dwarf trees in bloom. In the winter you could look into the greenhouse with its abundance of flowers.

The exhilaration of being young and walking fast on a New York City Street, in your prime—and being without doubts, IN LOVE, cannot be described—only felt, and the whipped cream of it all: Spring in wartime New York!

Joan's husband left; Joan breathed a sigh of relief. Now I moved back to #28 also with a feeling of relief, but with the expectation of Jack's return, now out of the service on medical discharge, back to Columbia. He had obtained a job at the *Lowell Sun* in the Sports Department, doping out horses, also writing about baseball, his favorite team sport for spring, but he was anxious to get back to me.

Joan and I started to search in earnest for our second apartment, reading the newspapers, putting notices on the Columbia bookstore board near the Lion's Den. I met Joan at the West End Bar one early spring morning. We started to pore over the ads. I had a beer and Joan had a Kummel. Geraldine Lust sat down with us. She was a day student at Barnard and liked to hang around with Joan and me because of all the fellows that were friends of Jack's and two "good looking" girls who always had men around.

We asked Gerry if she knew any places to rent. She said a professor was going into the service and his family was going back home to Des Moines. She didn't know of any other possibilities nor could she think of any other leads.

Gerry was from the South—kind of dumpy and immature. She was absolutely crazy about men—and drove us nuts. Anyway, she wanted to share our apartment. We wanted to know how much she could swing, moneywise. Gerry said maybe $25.00 per month. That was a lot so Joan and I looked at each other and Joan said we'd let her know, depending on what we could get—size, money, and all. In the meantime, we had marked off a few ads. We got up to go and said, "So long, see you later."

As we were going, Mad Grover, a real eccentric genius who had an eye on Joan, wanted to tag along. We hurried for Gerry would notice and follow. We started down towards Riverside Drive, took a right, and went into a building right in back of the West End. Joan stopped here every other day because she knew the "super" and he was asking other "supers" about vacancies. We rang his bell. He was an old man with a thick foreign accent. He gave Joan a piece of paper with an address on it. We said thanks and off we went to 112th Street and Riverside Drive. We went into this building, rang the "super's" bell, and he came out to greet us. He took us up in the freight elevator. We didn't like the apartment. "No Pets!"

Grover, Joan, and I strolled down to the Hudson River. It was a warm Sunday. The Julliard students would be gathering in Riverside Park to sing. This was one of the most beautiful things about Sundays. Jack would never miss their singing; their voices were glorious and they sang everything from classical to popular songs from the Civil War to the present. A statue of Ulysses S. Grant, mounted on his horse, looked down upon us. His tomb was off in the distance, close enough that you could almost see it if it weren't for the trees. They sang World War I songs. It was very moving and made me lonesome for Jack.

We finally found our new home at 421 W. 118th Street, Apartment #62. It was here that Williams S. Burroughs came into our lives, along with Herbert Huncke, Allen Ginsberg, Lucien Carr, and John Kingsland. Joan's final, most eventful phase of her life had begun.

JAN KEROUAC

from Baby Driver

The park, Tompkins Square, was a lush night green of leaves calling with mystery and romance through the smell of the river and the pulse of congas—a dark umbrella of vegetation for refugees from concrete and misplaced victims of puberty. It provided a temporary illusion of sanctuary, all the more attractive for being in the middle of the city, like a tuft of mold tucked in the groove of a boulder.

It was in that park that Charlotte introduced me to Paul Orlov. He was a tall slim fellow wearing an English cap and brown hexagonal shades, disguising large, fascinating hazel eyes. High on something at the time, he was elatedly dancing around looking for 7UP signs—obsessed with the logo.

I was instantly taken by him. This was my cosmic brother, all wrapped up in crazy obsessions that I understood implicitly. He was just young enough at heart, and I was just mature enough for us to meet halfway; however, in years I was twelve and he was twenty-two and when my mother heard about this she balked. My independence had flown me a bit too far from the coop. She let me know that she didn't condone our relationship, but the attraction was so powerful between us that there was nothing she could really do. I don't know how else to describe the ambience of that time, except that it was *magical*. Even before we took acid together there was stardust sprinkled in the streets for us to walk on. It hadn't been defined yet into sunbursts and arabesques, but they were there waiting to take shape.

Valentine's Day, 1965, two days before my thirteenth birthday, was the day I first took LSD. It was a Friday, and the first time I intentionally played hooky. Early in the morning I'd left my building as usual with looseleaf notebook, plaid pleated skirt, and bobby socks, and went straight to Paul's house at 99 St. Mark's Place. I was always glad to leave the disintegrating halls and footworn steps of 709 East Sixth Street and be enveloped by the neat unsqualorous tile and quiet of his building. After climbing breathlessly to the top floor, I was rewarded by the sublime order of his apartment, the exotic yet domestic universe we'd created of paintings, perfectly rolled joints, and canned chili dinners imbued with dream tones of the Modern Jazz Quartet.

I greeted Paul like another self. His mouth when we kissed was a complementary mouth—it fit every contour, as did his mind. It was so obvious that we should be together, *so* obvious that no one else could see. On this morning he had come to the door with a bouncy elfin secretiveness, and after thrice bolting it behind me he said, "Look what we have," and took out of the refrigerator a tray of closely paved sugar cubes, each with a small brown stain in the center.

"Hmmm. . . ." I replied, setting down my books and scrutinizing the curious cubes.

"Well?" He laughed with a playful twinkle. "Shall we?"

We wasted no time picking out our consecrated wafer. We sat down at the round table where we did all of our drawings and poems, smoking grass and hash into the night atop hilariously inspired universes. Paul habitually arranged neat clusters of things, like his hexagonal, root-beer-colored sunglasses placed on their case, which was on top of a folded scarf, next to a carving of a monkey, and a candle which was surrounded by dominoes and more trinkets. On the wall hung an old-fashioned one-day-at-a-time-type calendar which was permanently opened to November 22—Paul's birthday, but also the date of Kennedy's assassination. It was a kind of altar to a God of Objects.

We stared for a while at the sugar cubes and then into each other's eyes until the right moment erupted, and with an inaudible *pop*, we popped them in. He'd already had a few trips and was now sharing the spell with me. In about half an hour the elastic gelatin was breathing inside me like stellar yeast. I found myself on the floor marveling over a labyrinth of Persian rug designs. They had become three-dimensional and were writhing beneath the floor as well as above. My hands were enmeshed in wriggling jeweled spaghetti. This kneading of the rug was a highly purposeful thing to be doing; it seemed everything had to be tended like magic dough.

The next thing I knew, we were out on the street feeling quite unusual and Paul was hailing a cab. The idea that we were going to see a movie, having taken acid, had seemed like a logical program of entertainment earlier, but now that we were high it was rather incomprehensible. The cab sped uptown, swerving and dipping into manhole depressions with springless jolts that made us think we would go right through the chassis and onto the pavement. We were two wild creatures peering out of steamy windows. My Persian rug designs had followed and were now spiraling along the blacktop.

Inside the theater, *That Man From Rio* was playing. Jean-Paul Belmondo leapt into one car after another, and I could hardly make him out behind the thick barrier of pastel stars in my head. Soon they covered the whole screen with their swirling mass, like bits of proto-plasm floating on the surface of your eyes. I crawled up to the lobby to buy some candy after a while, and spent a great deal of time spilling silvery coins all over the red carpet in front of the vending machine. They all looked foreign, with strange letters and symbols, and I couldn't figure out which ones to put in. I must have decided on something, because I returned with some candy.

The candy added a whole new dimension to things. With each bite of chocolate, a fresh spray of fairy beams would fly through the high dark-vaulted ceiling—chocolate diamonds, coconut quasars, almond hearts. With our heads leaned back against the seats, we were staring straight up at a display of hallucinatory fireworks. Slowly, as if for a joke, the hearts began to take over—valentines with banners up there and greetings written in lysergic longhand. I turned to Paul and managed to form the words through my aphasia: "Do . . . you . . . see . . . those . . . val . . . en . . . tines . . . tooooo?" He nodded, and for the first time we noticed each other's saucer eyes, illuminated by flashes of Brazilian sun on Belmondo's windshield and by the glow from the electric pink ribbons dancing above. Wordless messages oozed out of Paul's pupils and we made our way out, stumbling over the rows of sleeping seats. We walked in the daylight of busy uptown Manhattan, and like bats, needed to hide somewhere. We found St. Patrick's Cathedral to be the perfect spot. But beholding all the beautiful stained glass, my eyes couldn't comprehend it, as if the LSD hallucinations were jealous of anything that subtracted from their own splendor.

In another cab going downtown we held hands, or paws it seemed—clammy paws of misplaced animals. When I looked into Paul's eyes I saw the most amazing vulnerability—dilated tar pits cradled in exhausted lids and trembling lashes.

There was more hooky-playing and acid-taking in the weeks that followed, and I even went to school high, getting a new perspective on my beloved Hunter. When I did my Latin homework it always wound up decorated with ballpoint paisley, practically camouflaging the words on the page. In math class I drew Egyptian eyes and five-pointed stars on the blackboard and argued with the teacher that a circle couldn't have 360 degrees if there were infinite points in space. I *knew*, because I could see them everywhere at that very moment. The more I played hooky, the more adept I became at forging my mother's excuse notes.

It was a very tenuous time, a time of manic inspiration, strug-gling to be independent before my time. I'd sit and brood for hours in my cluttered blue room with its CAUTION sign, silver steam pipe and purple cat curtain respirating slowly in the window from cool soot breaths from a brick canyon . . . beckoning. The black-painted glass pane in my door was acquiring a diagonal crack from my mother's slamming it in frustration. We had terrible arguments that accidentally turned into fights, all over my desire to be with Paul. And I was dimly aware that my mother had been pregnant and had given birth to a new baby brother—David—who resided in a crib in the front room. I stared at him once while on acid, at his amazing bald head with its network of veins like the canals of Mars.

That summer of '65 a lot was brewing. It seemed hotter and more humid than ever, and there seemed to be gang wars almost every night down in the street. Leaning out a cool windowsill, I could watch the two warring gangs approach each other from opposite avenues and converge in the middle with a tremendous clash of brass knuckles, chains, knives, sticks, and sometimes even guns. The cops would cruise the avenues but dared not interfere. Only when it was over and several bodies lay scattered over the pavement would they move in cautiously and drag them away.

In the daytime, the same was true of the fire hydrant jets. Some of the big boys had special wrenches to open them with, and as soon as the morning started to swelter, the water was unleashed and hordes of squealing urchins ran out to play in the rivers that coursed through the gutters. Mothers washed out diapers in it, people of all ages who didn't have running water in their buildings washed their hair in it, you name it. It was like a tropical tributary of the East River, this miniature Ganges of East Sixth Street.

Tough kids opened both ends of beer cans and took turns using them to channel the gushing torrent from the hydrants into open tenement windows, trying to see who could hit the highest one. It was so hot that everyone's windows were open, so you just hoped they wouldn't pick yours, otherwise you'd be sitting in your living room sweating and fanning yourself when in would burst a whoosh of water all over the floor.

Every car that ventured onto that street was in for a wash, and woe to anyone who forgot to roll up his windows. About every two hours the cops would routinely come along, and everyone, guilty or not, would disappear from the street like crumbs sucked up by a vacuum cleaner, leaving the hydrant gushing and the street ridiculously empty. The cops would turn it off and leave again with wry hopeless expressions on their faces, probably off to another street to cap another hydrant. The second they were out of sight, everyone would reappear, with almost slapstick timing.

Paul and I spent most of the time uptown in Central Park or wandering God knows where, watching induced visions from our black-lacquered lenses. I actually could see the trees breathing, etiolating in verdant blooms. Sidewalks studded with letters—semiprecious alphabet soup—danced before my feet, spelling out partial messages of cosmic import.

One day we started our enchanted itinerary earlier than usual at Paul's house, after watching the sun come up from the roof and drawing things in colored chalk on the warm tar. We had already taken acid and were waiting for it to take effect. It seemed to be a longer wait than usual, but after about forty-five minutes it crept up, tagging us from behind like a playful goblin.

The first thing I noticed was a shadowy blue corridor splitting open before me lined with what looked like Egyptian mummy tombs, all of them whispering in special LSD language—an untranslatable flutter of spectral wings. These whispers were telling me not to reveal what I was being shown, that it was an ancient secret. I turned to my right and another such corridor split open, silently, but with a distinct vibration like moving rock. It was lined with more sarcophagi, each one decorated with the carved bejeweled face of its owner. Finally, I had turned to all four directions, and found myself to be in the middle of a crossroads where these tunnels converged.

I looked at Paul, who was sitting in a princely attitude in his antique Early American chair. He rose and held up his hand—the palm and five fingers appeared so perfectly formed—and I saw a message of some sort in the gesture, although he probably had totally different things going on in his mind. I stared reverently and nodded. I understood.

Moving statically to the next room, I perceived the large, square, blue electric fan on the floor. It was sucking in all my stonelike hallucinations and whizzing them up, returning them to the air in billowing rainbow ribbons. I watched, mesmerized by this, as the Staple Singers sang "Give Me That Old-Time Religion."

The whole apartment had been transformed into the interior of some palace on the Nile. Palms were being waved by fabricated servants who were actually part of the wall. When the ageless gospel strains of the record stopped, I heard water dripping in paradisaical tones somewhere—most likely from the leaky kitchen faucet—but it sounded to me like primeval droplets in the Garden of Eden.

We floated down the stairs and into the street where all the buildings had become monuments and pyramids. This LSD had the power to distort cubiform structures into rhombuses, bend squares into triangles, split stone, solidify fire, and liquefy wood. What would it do next? Strolling through the park on that tropically warm, sensual day, all the potential for pleasure—visual, tactile, and otherwise—had been unleashed upon us. The world was turning its exquisite sides to us as if we were privileged spectators at a galactic beauty contest.

Somehow we ran into my mother and sisters shopping and followed them, which was very out of character for us. On Avenue B a fire engine went by, nearly devastating my very soul . . . such a mad spectacle of shining RED machinery and blasting noise I'm surprised it didn't wipe all the Egyptian visions off the face of my mind. After it passed, shaking the blacktop, I stood on the curb shivering like a baby sapling after a blizzard, and rearranging what few brain cells I had left.

On they marched and we zigzagged to the supermarket, with its garish aisles of multicolored cans and boxes. Of course in all this there was no resemblance to anything remotely Egyptian, but I thought I had already died and been buried in the Necropolis . . . this was some kind of Purgatory.

The shopping was done, no thanks to us, and next we wound up in the waiting room of the welfare office. I think my mother was taking advantage of our dubious presence to get a lot of things done while we babysat my sisters. But we weren't watching them very closely. All I remember watching was a yellow stucco wall where the whole history of Egypt unfolded before me in moving hieroglyphics. The ochreous plaster was melting and re-forming itself into men pulling ropes, rowing boats, pushing huge rocks, gazing at stars, and queens standing by rivers, and women having babies one after the other like pelvic totem poles of birth.

Paul and I stayed together all day near my mother and sisters, as if ignoring any implications that he was too old for me, or that we shouldn't be together. Our earthly bonds had been transcended anyway, and we meant no ill-will to my mother. Quite the contrary, we were fairly humming with untamed cosmic love.

Dinner was hamburger and a salad, but neither Paul nor I was able to eat the meat. We tried, but ended up smashing pieces of it between our fingers, agog at the wiggly warm steaming substance, reeking with a scent that sang of pain, strangely appealing yet repelling too. After a few small bites it felt impossible going down, as if we were chewing up our own hands.

Repairing to my room with a candle, we dined on crisp lettuce leaves dipped in oil and lemon juice, eating them one by one with our fingers like Romans dangling bunches of grapes. We took turns with the leaves, sending messages in crunching sounds accompanied by glances from our inky irises in the liquid gold glimmer of the flame.

Paul left after a spell, taking his half of our enchanted world away with him. I remained in my room all night and every time I closed my electrified eyelids, there in front of me was a stone face mirroring mine, smack before my Third Eye, attached indelibly everywhere I turned. It was the crystallization of those corridors I'd seen at the beginning of the trip. The candle sighed and melted, oozing yellow lava all over the bookcase, and I sat masking and unmasking a sphinxian alter-self as the last droplets of LSD filtered through my bloodstream. At dawn, chalky violet embraced the window and I finally drifted off to a weight-less sleep as pink-tinged clouds marched over the rooftops dressed as phantom princes.

There was a week that summer, toward the end of August, when Paul took acid every day. I had never done more than a dose at a time and was a little worried about him. He wasn't sleeping or eating, just flitting about in one big hallucination. He had become Identity Man, a character out of one of his own cartoon strips.

It was time for an appointment with his psychiatrist, and instead of avoiding or forgetting it, like I expected he would, he was eager to go there—he had all sorts of wonderful truths to tell his doctor. I went up with him to Metropolitan Hospital, and tried discouraging him several times without success.

In the lobby Paul did magic tricks for me, flicking his cigarette butt into the air and catching it in his cap, saying, "Now you see it, now you don't!" He did this over and over with different objects, smiling black twinkles from his eyes, astonished at his own feats. I knew how he felt and laughed along with him, recalling my own recent highs. But the psychiatrist would *not* understand, I kept telling Paul, who was so enraptured by his wizardry that he wouldn't listen.

I was allowed in with him when he was called. Paul immediately started in on the man, spouting obtuse witticisms and displaying his Emperor's New Sorcery. After a few minutes of this, the doctor left the room and returned with a nurse who handed Paul a small white paper cup. The cup had a pill in it which they told him to take. "Thanks!" he said gleefully, and put it in his pocket.

"No, we want you to swallow it," they insisted, at which point Identity Man defiantly flipped it into the air and when it landed, crushed it into the carpet with his heel, chanting, "Now you see it, now you don't!"

Next thing I knew, Paul was being taken on a tour of the building, and I waited for him in the office. A half hour had elapsed when I was told I could see him. The doctor took me up in the elevator to the thirteenth floor, and there was Paul in a striped bathrobe, looking very confused behind a glass barrier. He'd become part of his own vanishing act: *Now you see him, now you don't.*

from Trainsong

In September I was offered a job as an extra in *Heartbeat*, a movie about my father's ménage à trois with the Cassadys. One smog-laden morn, John drove me down to the shoot on Fourth Street. The Acropolis Café was just the place for a beat generation coffeehouse scene: a Greek restaurant in downtown L.A., unchanged since the thirties, its bare green walls easily took on the ambience of San Francisco in 1956.

In the wardrobe trailer, I sat right next to Nick Nolte, who was having his face expertly plastered at the same time I was having my hair firmly yanked up into a tortuous pompadour. I had a half-pint carton of milk in my lap, and when he squeezed behind me to get out, I pulled the flimsy director's chair up closer to the dresser to give him more room and spilled the milk on my lap. Luckily I was still wearing my own jeans. That was just the beginning. Later, outside, I met John Heard, who was to play my father, and Sissy Spacek, who was cast as Carolyn Cassady. We all had plenty of time to gab in the sun, like children dressed up for Sunday School—metamorphosed into stiff anachronistic manikins. I helped John practice his Jack lip, showing him one of the few things I knew about my father, which was the way he stuck out his lower lip, easy for me because I had inherited it. And Sissy and I struck up a conversation, trading childhood stories: hers about Texas, in a husky drawl which I found to be hypnotic, and mine about New York. Meanwhile hoards of L.A. weirdos were pestering Sissy about her role as Carrie and asking her for autographs, and some energetic photographer was snapping rolls of photos of the two of us sitting on a packing crate.

Finally, we were allowed to enter the Acropolis Café. Yards of thick black cyclopsian equipment were dragged and wheeled into the cool, high-ceilinged place, where everyone again waited and waited— this time sitting at tables. Then the holy trinity took their places next to the biggest cyclops. The rest of us were supposed to comprise the background, blurred anonymous figures. My job was to sit at a table where two guys were playing a game of chess: to follow their moves like a cat, then to look mildly bored and giggle occasionally in my slinky beige crepe dress with pearl embroidery and massive shoulder pads, three-tone high heels, and heavily sprayed hairdo. We were all told to puff like mad on our Camel straights to produce a thick, smoke-filled atmosphere, and females were instructed to kiss a red blotch of lipstick onto the ends of their cigs.

Nick Nolte startled us all with a bout of spasmodic stamping and shuffling of feet, and drumming on the table, a curiously dynamic way of clearing his head—or, perhaps, essence of Neal Cassady popping through? Then he'd shout, "Okay, ready!" and the time machines would roll.

Either I was slowly asphyxiating from the Camel smoke, or toxic chemicals in the makeup were infiltrating my bloodstream, but gazing up at the lazily revolving black fans in the pressed waffle tin ceiling—I forgot *everything*. All I knew was, there I was, Camel burning in the ashtray, surrounded by outdated housewives in pincurlers and scarves, in some strangely contrived bubble of time when I wasn't even *born* yet. I experienced a disturbing notion: could I be my own mother? And who is that dark-haired man over there pouting in baggy blue pants, talking about poetry to the blond couple: My father? My absentee husband? Where is this? California? Colorado? New York? What is this? Who am I?

"—I'm drunk, in the middle of the afternoon—" The husky golden Texas twang of the blond woman brought me reeling back to reality, the dubious reality of a movie set, spotlights softened with smoke spirals. . . . *Oh, that's right, I'm just an extra. Extra, extra read all about it!*

That afternoon I wandered home up Hollywood Boulevard in milk-stiff pants, with spray-stiff hair, feeling like some kind of a doll that had been starched and pressed flat, two dimensional, and escaped from a toy-store window. But I also felt fulfilled in a funny way, as though the Neptunian illusions of Tinseltown had wrapped my father in Technicolor celluloid and brought him back to me special delivery, straight into my arms.

from **Nobody's Wife**

Chapter 19

On a sloppy wet evening in early April, I came home from work tired and worn, to find Jack staring unhappily and silently at his typewriter.

I had found a better waitressing job at the new Brass Rail on Park Avenue and 41st. All the help was new, including Puerto Rican busboys just off the plane, some speaking no English at all. For two weeks prior to opening we were trained in heavy silver service, tray on the shoulder. I laughed aloud on the night of the grand opening when the first two letters on the neon sign failed to light up. From that night on, I would always remember that restaurant as the red neon "ASS RAIL."

Jack seemed to have been locked in some struggle with *On the Road* through my whole training period. He wasn't writing, and he wasn't talking much, either. He asked broad, grasping questions about style, about structure. They seemed thoroughly irrelevant to me. Neal was spontaneous. The words should simply come out. They should spill onto the page without control, finding style and structure in the telling.

I sat down across from Jack and looked tiredly back at him. "What was it like, Jack?" I finally asked, after a long silence.

"To be on the road with Neal?"

"Yes, what happened, what really happened?"

I started asking questions. Questions about Neal, about traveling, cities, trains, New York, Mexico, cars, roads, friends, Neal, Neal, Neal, and Neal.

"Jack," I asked him again, "what really happened? What did you and Neal really do?"

The questions, after a time, seemed to ignite some spark in Jack. He went back to his typewriter, and now he typed with accelerating speed, pounding keys, late into the night. When I got up in the morning, I saw that the clothes he had dropped on the floor were soaked with sweat. And I saw that there were feet and feet of the teletype roll, filled with dense typescript, hanging off the back of the typewriter now.

I was glad Jack was writing again. It improved his mood immeasurably. I knew it was ironic that I acted as his muse and his inspiration when his writing had always been so unimportant, even unreadable, to me. But it was such a relief to have him focused on something other than his own boredom and selfish needs.

For the next few weeks, I became accustomed again to sleeping while Jack typed. I only woke if it stopped suddenly. That happened one night, May 10, 1951, and the consequences would change both our lives forever.

Jack was in his bathrobe, behind the screen that surrounded his desk, typing furiously. The typing stopped. I opened my eyes, and almost immediately he emerged.

"Quick!" he said, dropping his bathrobe and pulling the covers off me. Now a brief argument ensued: spontaneity vs. preparedness. Spontaneity won, and the diaphragm stayed buried with the socks.

Two minutes later Jack rolled over and went to sleep. I knew I wasn't responsible for his arousal, and I got up to see what was in the typewriter. I found my answer in his description of Terry, the Mexican girl he knew in California, and the pity he felt for her. Remembering other occasions when I hadn't been able to understand what precipitated his sudden inspiration, it all hung together. There was always an element of the pathetic, or the down-trodden, or abject poverty and misery, either in the conversation or in something or someone he'd seen. I had never allowed him to see anything of that sort in me. I would not acknowledge my own weakness or pain and I never cried. So I had nothing to do with his arousal. I was merely the receptacle.

This was the time, though, that the receptacle turned out not to be empty.

In late June I began to think I was pregnant. Apprehensively, unhappily, I told Jack. He was sure I was mistaken, but he sent me to Ti-Nin's obstetrician, and the doctor confirmed my suspicion.

Jack was still unbelieving. He couldn't accept the idea. Not that he didn't want children. It just wasn't the right time. The book wasn't finished. He talked about Neal's irresponsibility, bringing all those kids into the world without making any provision for them.

"Nine months is enough time for two people to prepare for a baby," I answered him. "I can work till my seventh month, anyway."

"The preparation should have been before the fact. Where was your diaphragm?"

"It was that night you wouldn't let me get up," I let him know.

"That's no excuse. A woman should always be prepared."

"That would be ridiculous, Jack, considering how seldom there's a need."

He gave me one of his dark looks and asked, "How far along are you? Did the doctor say?"

"About seven weeks."

"That's early!" he said. "We can get something done. It would be cheaper in the long run."

I shook my head.

"What's the matter with you?" He was exasperated.

"It's out of the question, Jack."

"Look, this isn't the dark ages. What are you afraid of? The legality? The morality?"

I shook my head again. I knew this child inside me, felt I had known her before I was born, and I knew she was staying with me. I just wasn't going to talk about it, except to say, "I'm going to name this kid 'Spontaneity.' "

"That's not very funny," Jack said glumly.

There followed two weeks of thick, troubled impasse. It boiled over in Jack late one night as I came through the door, carrying my shoes in my hand.

"All right," he insisted, seemingly taking up some angry conversation he'd already been having with me in his mind. "I've decided. Having a baby is out of the question."

I wasn't about to listen to an ultimatum. I threw my own back at him. "No, Jack. What's out of the question is an abortion."

He glared at me, eyebrows crushed together in indictment of my willfulness. "You always think you can have it whatever way you want. Well, this time you will have to choose. Do you want a husband or do you want a baby?"

I laughed. "You mean, which baby do I want? The husband or the one in here?" I patted my belly.

Jack sputtered.

"There is no choice! Jack, this is too easy. This baby is mine. It's the only thing in this life that belongs to me. If you want to move out, move out. It won't bother me a bit. I don't need two babies!"

I looked then at Jack. That vein over his temple was throbbing ominously, looking like a swollen river. I realized that although he hadn't made any gestures, any threats to me, that I was stooped in a cowering position. My words masked my fear.

The shock of my own vulnerability swarmed over me with a wave of panic, and I felt almost physically sick. I was no longer responsible only for myself, my seemingly indestructible self, never ill and unable to feel pain. Now I was two. Now there was another with me, and her safety was my charge, and her health depended only on mine. My long-running feelings of detachment were a thing of the past. I was both literally and figuratively attached to this child. It was beyond the point of decision.

Jack went to Lucien's without even taking his slippers.

I asked for more hours at work. I would need every cent I could make now. I had three good friends at work, all Puerto Rican, and one night we all went to Spanish Harlem to dance. I insisted on taking the bus home, not wanting to spend money for cab fare. Angelo, a Brass Rail busboy, waited with me in the rain and rode downtown with me.

He saw me to my door and I asked him to come in. I knew that he'd heard about my husband's book, and that he admired writers and poets. But Angelo's upbringing had been strict in regard to moral conduct, especially where married women are concerned, and he was reluctant to come inside. I assured him that he was welcome in my home, that Jack was gone, and that it would be my pleasure to make him a cup of coffee and show him the copy of *The Town and the City* that Jack had given me the first day we met.

We debated in the rain. Finally Angelo decided the coffee was too tempting, and he would come in for a moment. I put the pot on and showed him Jack's picture on the cover of *The Town and the City*. Angelo spoke no English. I opened the book and read from the first page, translating the text for him.

Suddenly, we heard knuckles rapping at the door. Angelo ran, intuitively, to the window. It was stuck, and while I shouted to him that there was no need to worry, Jack yelled from outside, "What's going on in there?"

Jack used his key to unlock the door, and he hurled it open. The minute the door budged, Angelo dashed out under Jack's arm. Jack jumped back, then, "What was that all about?" he asked furiously.

I rescued the coffee and told Jack where we'd been, how I had asked Angelo in, and why he was afraid. It was obvious from the order of the room that nothing amiss had transpired. There wasn't so much as a wrinkle in the bedspread. But Jack's eyes had lit up by this point.

"How do I know you haven't been running around with that spic for the past two months?"

"How about, because I only met him two weeks ago."

"Or some other spic! How do I know what you do with your time when I'm out?"

I wanted to lean into his face and unleash the most unearthly scream I could muster, but instead I ground my teeth together and seethed. "Did you come over to get your stuff?" I asked in a white fury. "Then get it! And take your paranoia and type it onto a toilet paper roll and flush it down the toilet!"

I had given up. It was over, and I began to make plans to move back to my mother's house in Albany County. I felt a deep sense of failure, underneath the turmoil of every other emotion. I had failed to make any real human connection, of love or friendship or caring of any type. Jack hated me, and I felt completely indifferent. My love with Herb had ended in simple escape, but this unhappy marriage of mine would end in bitterness and enmity. And more and more, now, I began to think of Bill. I wished for his advice, the words of my big brother all but genetically. I mourned him in a way I had not at the time of his death; by feeling a deep sense of loss that he wasn't with me.

When Jack called and said that he wanted to talk one more time, and asked me to meet him on the rooftop of Lucien's building, I was stung with an anguished sense that he knew how much I missed Bill, and that he wanted to burn me with it until I cried out for mercy. The mere mention of the place embroiled me in memories of Bill, of chasing him across rooftops wrapped in sheets, of the way he would sometimes gaze across the buildings of his city.

But I wasn't willing for Jack to know how much it hurt, and I agreed to meet him there.

Standing in the warm night, waiting for him to arrive, I looked across the lights of New York and lost myself in a reverie. *Grandfather*, I murmured in my mind. *I had a beautiful, perfect web, and now it has been destroyed by the sunlight.*

Finally, Jack arrived. I had assumed we were going to talk about a divorce. But Jack had another question on his mind.

"What if I said you could have the baby? What then?"

I looked at him in the still night air for a long time, wondering. Is he giving me another chance at a bad marriage? Asking for another chance for himself? Or is the question purely hypothetical?

"I don't need your permission," I told him finally. "Or want it, either."

He turned on his heel and stalked downstairs. After a while I started down too. Passing by Lucien's door, I heard Jack shouting, "All right! I asked her! And she won't have me back! Now don't tell me that kid's my responsibility. I don't ever want to hear about it again."

And now I whispered to myself again as I hurried down the hall, this time to the big brother I'd found and then lost. *Bill*, I silently prayed. *Why did you ever bring us together? Why did you ever think it could work?*

Why did you leave me, Bill?

JOANNE KYGER

Tapestry

                    The eye
                    is drawn
                    to the Bold
                    DESIGN
                    the Border
                    California flowers
          nothing promised that isn't shown
                    Implements:
                    shell
                    stone
                    Peacock

....

          Waiting again
       What for

       I am no picker from the sea of its riches
       I watch the weaving, the woman who sits at her loom
What was her name?   the goddess I mean
Not that mortal one

                    Plucking threads
          as if they were strings of a harp

They are constructing a craft
    solely of wood
at Waka-no-ura, fishing village,
  a jewel quite naturally
from the blue of the farm house tile roofs.

              found on the southern coast.

The women pull by hand long strings
          of seaweed across the shore

it dries

                  At the other end of the town
              the hull of the boat rises

above the smaller houses

A little prince of a boy in a white knit suit
    stands with the others in a group on the beach

Watching us go by, we are strange.

                  The women bend over
the seaweed, wakame, changing its face to the sun.

It is lonely

I must draw water from the well   75 buckets for the bath

I mix a drink—gin, fizz water, lemon juice, a spoonful
                    of strawberry jam

And place it in a champagne glass—it is hard work
          to make the bath

And my winter clothes are dusty and should be put away

In storage.   Have I lost all values I wonder
          the world is slippery to hold on to

When you begin to deny it.

Outside outside are the crickets   and frogs in the rice fields

Large black butterflies like birds

The Hunt in the Wood: Paolo Uccello

The grey hounds go leaping into the woods
            the hunters behind them
and the trees have their lower branches cut
        So the men with their poles will not be struck
            and a horse has suddenly stopped
                on a ring of flowers the rider crying Ho
                    up to the sky
            Small figures way
back in the woods with the hounds shout
        The white hounds this way and that
        like bounding deer or rabbits
                    And the deer
here he is with the antlers,   by the pond
                        closed in upon
        They move from the dark of the wood
to the midst, the racing men and their ribbons
        and the deer rushed back towards them.

Waiting

        over the lilacs won't he   come home
    to at least rest tonight,   I want to see
the round car safe in the driveway, cinders
        and the moon over head

The persimmons are falling
early and rotten from the tree.
                    no time to attend the garden.
            where I go like a dandy
        is to the living room
                    and right to the heart of the matter.

From here   to here.
        how much are you going to do.
                    It occurred to me yesterday
people don't die at thirty.
                    But the bloom is gone.   all this
        awareness of a bloom to die.   what a sad time
when the point is clear and we settle down like ripe wheat
            the beginning business over.

            There reoccurs a dream
    of a large mysterious house, of women in turbans
                gigantic attics of rubbish
        a long staircase, mysterious inhabitors
        of closed off suites, marble fountains
            sneaking through the house
            in by the back way, I can't take over.

    The great house has strange furniture I'm unfamiliar with
                In a chair in the living room
    I don't know a thing, about what's around the corner.
    going up the staircase, knocking on the doors.

    The different preoccupations.   years and years
go by.   A bad crop of persimmons eaten with bugs
this year, a good one last.   And the wrinkles.
                Melting into the nice earth
        giving over life, giving it another child.

    'You've built this vast house. now explore it.'
        —Some people have well lived rooms.

The Pigs for Circe in May

I almost ruined the stew and Where
is my peanut butter sandwich I tore through the back of the c..
I could not believe
there was One slice of my favorite brown bread and my stomach and
I jammed the tin foil and bread wrappers into the stew
and no cheese and I simply could not believe
and you never
TALK when my friends are over.

This is known as camping in Yosemite.

Already I wish there was something done.
Odysseus found a stag on his way to the ship
I think of people *sighing* over poetry, *using* it,   I
don't know what it's for. Well,

Hermes forewarned him.   Can you imagine
those lovely beasts all tame   prancing around him?

She made a lot of pigs too.

I like pigs.   Cute feet, cute nose, and I think

some spiritual value investing them.   A man and his pig together,
rebalancing the pure in them, under each other's arms, bathing,
eating it.

And when the time came, she did right
let them go
They couldn't see her when she came back
from the ship, seating themselves and wept, the wind
took them directly north, all day
into the dark.
at least they were moving again

Sometimes I just go hobbling up and say
Just a little *Food*, please.   Usually a piece of bacon or toast
the coffee curling up in the pine groves of Yosemite.
There is a rock wall
in the night
animals and something hot and dank on the sand trail
in the sun;
waste

Odysseus went down and got his comrades

'Circe says it's ok to stay.'
                   And they were freely bathed and wined.
She had a lot of maids and a staid housekeeper.
                       I mean, I admire her.   The white robes
and keeping busy
She fed her animals
wild acorns, and men crying inside

                   with a voice like a woman
         from the sun and the ocean
She is busy at the center, planning out great
stories to amuse herself, and a lot of pets,
       a neat household, gracious
            honey and wine
She offers.
              Purple linen on the chairs
        Odysseus mopes
'Oh I'll give you your bores back'   They weep to see each other
      a black ram
   and a young ewe and the ship to hell
where Persephone has left only one man with reason
              She doesn't hold them back
                  a young man dies
     that is his fault.
          And she asked him to stay
       climbing all day
        pushing
     strewn with boulders
          the great leap it makes
into space, giddy he rushes at her
    the roar he makes
         on the wide shelf bed
   they both watch over the edge

     and the Great Pigs waddle off in the sky—

FRAN LANDESMAN

The Ballad of the Sad Young Men

All the sad young men
Sitting in the bars
Knowing neon lights
Missing all the stars

All the sad young men
Drifting through the town
Drinking up the night
Trying not to drown

Sing a song of sad young men
Glasses full of rye
All the news is bad again
Kiss your dreams goodbye

All the sad young men
Seek a certain smile
Someone they can hold
For a little while

Tired little girl
Does the best she can
Trying to be gay
For a sad young man

Autumn turns the leaves to gold
Slowly dies the heart
Sad young men are growing old
That's the cruellest part

While a grimy moon
Watches from above
All the sad young men
Play at making love

Misbegotten moon
Shine for sad young men
Let your gentle light
Guide them home again
All the sad young men

"She" (for Hanja)

She so pretty, She so crazy
So delightful and so lazy
She make pictures, She make babies
All her life is full of "maybes"

She can light your darkest hours
She got visions, She got powers
Everything She makes unravels
Got no money, still She travels

She play cinderella
In fantastic rags
Pretty girls beside her
Look like well-dressed hags

She got beauty mixed with sadness
She make magic, She make madness
Read your hand or cure your fever
But her lovers always leave her

She so lovely, She so vicious
She do cooking so delicious
I could kill her, I could kiss her
When She go away I miss her

The Princess from Flatbush

She's got a bracelet from Cartiers and beauty and wit
She's got a dozen new lovers but none of them fit
She's got two eyes like black olives and very nice tits
She's just a Princess from Flatbush who stays at the Ritz

She came a long way from Brooklyn without a career
She's busy hiding and seeking and fighting her fear
She's got a house on the lakefront, a plum tree with plums
But all her elegant dinners still taste of the slums

She settled in Geneva beside a crooked man
Goes skiing in the winter and keeps her perfect tan

The crooked man has vanished and left her lots of bread
She's reading Krishnamurti to straighten out her head

She studied chess with a master and soon had him beat
But all her really good gambits she learned in the street
I go to faraway places and find far-out chums
But I remember her kisses that taste of the slums

Spring Can Really Hang You Up the Most

Spring this year has got me feeling
Like a horse that never left the post
I lie in my room staring up at the ceiling
Spring can really hang you up the most

College boys are writing sonnets
In the tender passion they're engrossed
But I'm on the shelf with last year's Easter bonnets
Spring can really hang you up the most

All afternoon those birds twitter-twit
I know the tune "This is love! This is it!"
Spring came along, season of song
Full of sweet promise but something wrong

Doctors once prescribed a tonic
Sulphur and molasses was the dose
Didn't help a bit. My condition must be chronic
Spring can really hang you up the most

All alone the party's over
Old man Winter was a gracious host
But when you keep praying for snow to hide the clover
Spring can really hang you up the most

It's Only a Movie

Don't cry baby, it's only a movie
It's only a picture show
Look and you'll see all the buildings are cardboard
That's only white sugar snow

Don't cry baby, that wound isn't bleeding
It's only tomato sauce
Don't get upset when they're pounding the nails in
It's only a cardboard cross

The wind machine keeps grinding
The thunder's just a drum
The film goes on unwinding
And will till Kingdom come

Don't cry baby, when somebody leaves you
The script called for him to go
Just remember it's only a movie
It's only a picture show

Why

Why is my every love a loss?
Why do our letters always cross?
Why do I always talk too much?
Why does it take so long to touch?

Why is my wisdom just a waste?
Why can't I rest alone and chaste?
Why won't I learn what time has taught?
Why am I always getting caught?

Why do I wear this foolish grin?
What would I do if I should win?
Should I be asking more or less?
Why is my every love a mess?

Homecoming

Somehow
The birds sound the same
When waking from a dream
In London or in San Francisco

Surely
The cats on the street
Are just as mean or sweet
In London or in San Francisco

So is the smell
Of morning coffee
But the colour
Is different

The grass is the same
It gets you just as high
So is the gossip and the blues
And the boys taste the same
They get you just as high
The only special thing
Is the colour of the sky

Where the Blues Begin

Have you come to the place where the days are black
And you've gone too far and you can't come back
And you pitch your tent on a cardboard range
And you sleep with creeps and your friends are strange
And your silver spoon turns to worthless tin?
Then you've come to the place where the blues begin

When there's nothing to do and you've done it twice
And you seem to live in a cave of ice
And you hear no hope in a ringing phone
And you haven't learned how to play alone
When the time is long and the laughs are thin
Then you've come to the place where the blues begin

Once life was funny, free and fast
In every act an all-star cast
They served you first but now you're last
How did you get so old so fast?

When you pray with your lips but the words won't come
And you beg for sleep like a bowery bum
And the hustler stares with his high-speed eyes
And you drown your fear in a glass of lies
When there's nothing left that you care to win
Then you've been to the place where the blues begin
Where the blues begin
Where the blues begin

All That Fall (for Ernie)

Blessings on the falling humans
Falling man and falling women
All that fall and feel the pain
Surely they will rise again

Blessings on the judge and jailors
Falling hearts and other failures
Dow-Jones Average, falling rain
All that fall will rise again

Blessings on the falling sparrow
Falling snow and falling dollar
Falling hopes and falling nations
All who fall on demonstrations

Blessings on the fallen angels
Falling friends and falling strangers
Falling stars and faithless men
Know dem bones will rise again

The Decline of the West

All the good tunes have been written
All the good songs have been sung
Somewhere a promise was broken
Long ago, when we were young

All the good words have been spoken
All the good wars have been fought
All the good scenes have been stolen
The big fish have all been caught

All the good weekends are over
All the good games have been played
May as well stay with your lover
The good moves have all been made

All of our bridges are burning
All the good songs have been sung
Somewhere we took the wrong turning
Long ago when we were young

Du.. of a Lady Female

Learn HOW to make love. Books help. Example: After reading a book about Life in Africa . . . that night was astonishing! The book did not SAY anything on love, it perfumed the mind. The MIND makes the love. The beefsteak is a local stop. One tested the mind with an early Pearl Buck bit on China. Ah! . . . night lasting far, far, far into the night.

Incense for love. A formula: A container which allows a small, long-burning candle to burn under it for hours. In this order, put into the container:

> bits of dried orange, tangerine and/or lemon peel about the
> size of postage stamps. Cloves. Whole nutmeg. Chinese or
> Japanese or East Indian incense. Frankincense, called Olibanum.

The peels heat up the rest slowly & releasing their oils give to the other odors a living quality.

Making love in a room kept perfumed, is like being inside a flower. For the purpose of love, sheets and coverings that touch the skin, ought to be silk. Lacking it, fine linen. Last, cotton.

Put into your lover's mind a picture of the KIND of PERSON you feel he secretly thinks he is. Make him love himself & be dependent on you for it. Never arouse jealousy.

Feed him. Dont use rich meats or gravies. They clog his bowels. A man with a clogged bowel will take to drink. Fruits & fishes, grains & vegetables. Give him the purest water possible, to drink.

No high or harsh tones of voice. He is more sensitive than you, to them. He's got a better sense of hearing & smell. Dont cry for yourself except by yourself. It acts on his nerves like a rockdrill. If you GOT to cry, do it for him. Example: DONT say: "poor, poor, little baby, you are under-privileged." Tell him: "when I think of all the sufferings that befall a male in this world of survival and chance . . . I could weep." Then you can cry. You'll have him weeping with you.

With incense burning the house will smell so exotic that your skin by contrast must smell like a piece of ripe fruit. Boil cucumbers with apple skins as fragrance for bath water. Perfumed soaps irritate the sensitive noses of the males. Rub orange or lemon oils into your skin. Against the heavy perfumed air of your bed chamber you'll smell like something good to eat.

Dont offer him a monotonous diet of movement or caresses. If you kiss him Friday . . . make him wait until Sunday for another. Dont scorn any way to make love. This is not the century for prejudice at any degree of life. Love him as if his ancestors were watching.

Alternate WITH MODERATION between excessive attention & affection to friendly chill indifference & languid movements. If you have put the right picture in his mind, of his own powerful maleness, you wont need anything else to keep his attention. Never, never, never tell him anything that puts a picture in his mind that you dont want to happen; because it will! Example: DONT say: "I bet you looked at all the girls on the bus today." Say: "I bet every chick on that bus looked at my pretty baby." Keep his mind on him.

In your love talking put a picture in his mind of something wildly adventurous, suiting his male nature. The Foreign Legion. International Jewel Smuggling. Stalking Through Africa. Tiger hunting in India. The High Imperial Presence of Ancient Cathay. The result, my sisters, will be this: you'll have no mere male, standing on his head repairing speedometers of automobiles, or a counter of monies, no indeed! You'll have the bravest Foreign Legionnaire of them all & he'll treat you with the extreme aroused interest of a male used to being predatory, a fine rapacious beastie.

Offer him a drink after such wild flights of fancy. Dont tell him what it is. His sensitive male nature makes him rebel against any act or word suggesting "mothering." Dont talk too much. Crush poppy seeds, boil them & add to the fresh juices of oranges or limes or lemons. Watermelon juices are good. The juice of celery and/or lemon & onion quiets the nerves.

Dont talk to him about anything but himself. Example: Never say . . . "I wonder if flying saucers are real?" Say: "I wonder what you'd do in a flying saucer, gone out of control, in outer space?" He'll make them real for you.

Practice honor. Fraternise with other females. Build a code of behaviour.

NEVER COVET OR FLIRT WITH THE MALE OF ANOTHER FEMALE. IF I CAN IMPRESS THIS LAW UPON YOU . . . I CAN PROMISE YOU . . . YOU WILL ONCE MORE RULE THIS WORLD.

If another female even EYE BALLS your male, do this:

Raise your voice. Warn her LOUD, CLEAR, FIRM, PLAIN, SPE-CIFIC. Say: "you low BITCH get your nose out of him or I'll ruin you." She will usually slink off. You will take her varnish of curls & lipstick away by calling her precisely what she is in the act of doing. Also no man of dignity likes the feeling of female dogs smelling him.

Should he complain that you're no lady, Sister, LET him go. He aint about to be your man, he's his mamma's. If losing him means death to you . . . kill him. For some females, those of slender bones and throats with little-Venus shapes & minds of tragedy, soft floating hair that goes misty in the rain, for such as these who pine & die for their male . . . DONT BOTHER. That bit was fine *last* century. Get him out of his flesh-drawers & deal with his spirit. It is against the law precisely because of this. What did you think those males made those laws about? By your nature you'd die anyhow. Take him with you, and teach him out there. It will also teach him to know who you are before he messes with your kind.

Follow your ladyGROWL with a ladyPURR to restore peace. After calling her a bitch, it might be nice to quote Mr. Lowercase Cummings: Say to the room at large: "you lovely things, now I see where Mr. Cummings was when he wrote:

> 'when faces called flowers float out of the ground.' "

If she aint bothered by your voice & you have to fight, the way to do it is this:

Let out a primitive hate yell. Lunge at & on her with full weight, push her down while you claw her face so she raises her hands to it. Once down, sit on her chest, pin her arms under you, put both hands in her hair, pull it hard & bang her head up & down on the ground. Try not to kill her unless it is a battle to death. Dont lose. Act fast, count on shock. The males, when they come out of their shock, will feel obliged to stop you. Always go out prepared to fight for your male or stay home with him.

Battle dress: short hair. No jewelry on the ears, arms or throat. Wear jewelry in your hair, where it can fall out easily or on your ankles where it will be a further weapon. An easily ripped dress. A good hip or breast appearing during the fight also produces shock in the male & keeps him from stopping you. Flat sandal shoes. You can wear jewels on your shoes. NO STOCKINGS OR CORSETS & NOTHING UNNATURAL OR UGLY. IT WILL WORRY YOU ABOUT EXPOSING ARTIFICE. YOU WONT BE ABLE TO FIGHT.

When you first meet a renegade female that puts her vanity before the honor of the race of females, tell her she has such a tiny waistline she should wear a tiny, oh a very tiny corset like the French women do. Always keep a supply of long dangling earrings & choke-collar neck-laces, expensive & beautiful, to give as presents to such UNdesirable females. When you fight with her you can use them to choke her & pull her ears. Encourage her all you can, to wear heels & fancy clothes. Help her to paint herself prettily. Encourage her to preen & pose. Prepare her for the battle day when you meet in public. No female looks as silly after & during a fight as those fluttery fly-chicks with everything concentrated on their vanities. We no longer need them. My sisters, we are almost there.

Have or adopt children. They ARE the future. Raise them according to the female code. Let the male teach them what their bodies can do. You put the ideas into their minds.

Teach them:

Children are a female responsibility & should descend through her.

Marriage is not LEGAL BUT MORAL. Let the mother make it and/or break it. The mother of the married pair, that is, or both maws.

To laugh, sing, dance or exclaim in public without shame.

To SEE beyond local things like race, age, sex, class or religions.

Teach them to be suspicious of anything hidden or secret. Arouse their anger against it. Teach them to love the clear, the sunny, the true, the free & open.

To share what they have with anyone who needs or wants it. That will outdate stealing.

If a man kill another, enslave him to the murdered man's family.

To look for & respect people born with perfect senses of rhythm. These are natural leaders. They are as the heart & lungs of humanity.

Teach them to keep the generations in touch with one another. Send age groups that are the same, floating throughout the world. Get them to know & speak to one another. Let them discuss with their own generation what & how they will work together when they inherit the world.

Teach them that every race in the world is a necessary part of mankind & that all-together they make one. The race of man will die out when any part of it dies.

That everything in Nature works both to create or destroy. It depends on the shape they are put into, as to which they will do. Fear & hate produce terror & destruction. Benevolent love produces warmth & radiance.

Teach the females natural methods of aborting & redeem our race of women from the hands of the Abortionists with steel knives.

Teach them that the word "illegitimate" is meaningless. There is NO such thing as an illegitimate child.

San Francisco, 1959

JOANNA McCLURE

1957

Dear Lover,

Here on the eve of everything and humility,
The new shoes—the new tooth—
Can't quite fill the gap left
By Kruschev, the rally, the gas chamber,
The satellite beaming down from the moon.

Your nerves ajar,
Mine apart.
Ghostliness, the promise of a
Dark change, hovers
Without motion
Between us—

Blocking the beautiful love felt two nights ago
And renewed by this pressure—
The pleasure of its discovery still fresh
Again last night.

Where are we?
Why the pain—so sane
And yet without purpose,
our plight.

You say you are an American—of the continent—
But it doesn't help your twitching nerves
Or the discouragement of being here, now, at this time
Sat upon by the pressure of these lunatic affronts.

I come from dusty desert mountains
Where people only killed other people, bad people,
And rattlesnakes and deer to eat
And valued their horse and families.

I have only lately learned to wear pointed shoes
                                    with delicate straps
And realize the value of a pearl choker with

High delicate necklines and short black gloves
Topped by wild cropped blond hair.
And I am glad & would wear them through a war
If I had to.

But these are not the battles I choose
These are only discoveries, like last night's love,
Which I want to fill a lifetime with
In order to stand a symbol of the things I still
                                    believe in . . .
Desires for freedom, bodily beauty, tenderness,
        & your love & your Desire for change &
                Truth.
There isn't anyone on our side, just here
        where we stand.

And it's been too long
To make it all all right again.
I can't defend them anymore
Or, more painful, can not disengage
        from this time or place and have no
                                    desire
For any other time or place but my own.
A stubborn Determination born somewhere
                                    in the struggle.

I've turned down too many Gods to
Start inventing my own now
Or believe in yours either.

I only sit & wait & care for you
And worry—for I wanted to spend my life
Fighting with you . . . but
I wonder—what happens to us
When everything breaks apart.

My femininity is not willing to carry
        me along through sudden change.
I wanted to die slowly of old age.
The sliced lily plant, still green, hurts me.
I have no heart for wars I can't fight
Or bombs that destroy.

Sound Poem

Clet—loud upon his shoulder.
Pflut—soft, felt upon my back.
Wind throws leaves from trees
At us, the porch, the ground.

They rustle now across the boards,
While cliffs *shuzzle* down
Small bits of dirt, dust and twigs
Toward low still water now at rest.

The pool reflects back light,
Vibrates with the shimmer of surface motion.
Different depths, inactive activity—
A pointillist painting, quietly gone mad.

Ocotillo

Mesa Verde
Was red.

"Table top"
My mother said.

Young mind
Wrapped itself

Around the concept
Watching

Straight flat
Red mud road.

"Clay"
She said.

The mind did
Another turn.

My uncle's house
Appeared, alone

Stark center of
The mesa.

The wind howled
Making

Pallisade bagpipes,
A desert horn,

Of his
Ocotillo fence.

A Chinese Painting

The stairs,
Up the mountain,
Are delicately, barely visible.

A chicken looks at
  A butterfly looking at . . .
                              I think of Issa.

....

7–21–61

I dreamed I was an elf queen sleeping
In the forest in a wide orange nectarine
Contour belt—curled and uncurling.

Wolf Poem I

The wolf had amber eyes.
They caught me
Unaware—

My breath stopped short,
A little.
My heart freed itself.

A woman was
Destroyed by
Wolf love.

I give thanks
For my
Narrow escape.

Wolf Poem II

Wolves,
Yes, lean.

Wolves,
Yes, powerful.

This wolf—
Venerable also.

But without
Your eyes

Your eyes
Your amber eyes

I would be
Where I was

       yesterday.

Outside Tucson

The sound
Imprints itself,

Becomes
The web

Of my soul—
Coyote

They call
It.

Not enough
To describe
            the event.

30th Birthday—Haiku

The sound of the fire.
The orange flowers on long stems.
Why did I put the rugs down?

A Vacancy

An old unconsummated
Love . . . hangs sadly
In my thoughts.

When passion is gone,
The moment—unspent—
Stands silent, accusing,

An abortion, neither buried
Nor born—its space
A vacancy.

Hollywood

He sees frantic
       parasites on the dying body
         of a city.

I sleep
   in unreal sets
   and groan physically
     at unreal blood
      and violence.

I tiptoe through
   perversion
   violence,
Hit jealously head on,
   and blush at my
   stupidity,

Avoid the desk clerk
   and feel rich

Surrounded by

Three men from Mars.

For Michael, Stanley & Tom

More Blessed to Give

You
Gave
Me
    the clap.

What
Shall
I
    give you?

Some other
Man's
Ba
    by?

Or a
Hand
Full
    of crabs?

> and tom, the existentialiste, drives, off, in his
> white eldorado, top, down, too

suddenly   quite   reallynatural a maze of flowers appeared
bellowing proud as newborn bulls and shining they confirmed
the jigsaw order of surprised tomatoes, restless green beans
and cafeaulait all over eliot which i couldnt help but
before all tom made us laugh in that cambridge not too far
from lilacsyard cambridge hausfrau restaurant that oldtime
rollicking blue-eyed rednosed pretzle jumping thumping
sweet cream sour fish and course beer old germany land of
old germans mudd le of cambridge so suddenly it took a
minute to know and by then tom was under the table prac
tising his existentialism haha ORDERorder something ach
goot mun goot mun E? bad phone ehticks the night wore
indigestible stars WATCH THAT ANGELFISH see now billions
of stars have transcended o they are scarves winking
bright fureyus scarves up on the snowslide of moon
yes i'm looking listening looking listening no no not
for me at you tomtom haha but its not amusing altho its
altogether funny as heaven ah purgatorio tarsoap in a ten
year olds mouth

4 am

    and tom, the existentialiste, drives, off, in his white
    eldorado cadillacconvertible, top-down, too.

you, phoebusapollo

           do you
have a turnkey

           no?

door swinging open, your eye is a door
& open the door swinging open against your hands.

tout le monde est arrive.
                         no?

o do not falter, the rivers edge
is wrought-iron
&, having this far falln with no flashlight
hike your pants up once more regard/

     the morning-glory vine impacted in eyerayed
     morality withers & grows deadly,
                             a vacuum!
   light reaches
   it/like orange-rinds jutting out
   of a canvas
             & the view jolts,
   the viewers gone thru themselves, one another
   one another (beggars: with only alleys to screw in)

     You
   want more
            inebriate in staid drunken violet
   longitudes
               om   mane   padme   hum

yes, it is shine, a cloth to wrap the earth in
& youre not very holy,

devils turnstyle, you suspect nothing while fools
crouch at the base of the crosshumming vine break light
to kindle their own remains—

Hokusai & Moraff

for
      tui
tously met
on slippery brink
of mt. fuji out
side meditation hall
egos akimbo
utterly shocking in
rainbow collision
one had the tool
one had the bowl

Hokusai got drunk

one night with Li Po
fondling Korean
celadon bowls
they both mistook for
chrysanthemum women
shattering waves, what
old salts Hokusai and
Li Po   zen fresh
in Kyoto brothel
betting on who cld
come to the river
more often w/out
drowning in the
blaze
            of myth

Piscean Hokusai

you can tell by his fish
each its own center
vibrant each stroke
of the cross-hatching a wave
like that negative

space between lovers
inland new england style
contra-dancing
to an unknown caller's mastery

Moraff to Hokusai

i'm enamoured of you
you decomposed artifice
line by line
abrupt & brilliantly folksy
you were hawk circling
mt. fuji under rainbow
auspicious coincidence
of flesh, mind-heart &
the relative world
you paid attention to detail
no matter how painful
thrust off samurai mind &
became warrior w/out weapon
looked into own-mind
before history begins
you were gentle & you slipped
through the golden
links of the chain

Hokusai: HAI

Hokusai at Home

disgruntled, hung-
over, no work
accomplished, lifts
up spider fallen
into his cha-bowl
w/lacquered chopsticks.

the garden wall
stones flicker.

Craft

Leaning with the wind
like a sapling like a slender
one too young to hv borne fruit
thinking how could poetry take
the place of seriousness
he came toward me pungent as the grass burning
he smoked
laundry flapping its sheets panties denims bras
what an ordinary day i said to him out here
in the pines taking his joint in my hand
in my mouth
just for the surprise to him

2.

whitefaces rove or stand in ornery clusters
under elms dying of elm disease.
cowbirds, earth brown dull, pecking in manure
without sound.
the artist shifts her easel
in accord with light.
the cattle move so slowly her hand becomes one.

3.

the song & who's gone unnamed & gone & continues
it is the light & we materialize our flesh
a long poem, its many interruptions crushing the light
as we talk & touch into triple rainbow body body of light that we are
foolish enough to believe we are here where we are

poetics

Tremoring
in woodstove
gets me to
        leap
up
shut
   the draft

shape
of the sound
gets
   me also

The personal
arrives
      split-second
wise

I write
a personal poetry
& I know an artist
who sculpts
       intricately
skeletons
in miniature
     of large
     animals

He showed
me his
   ratskull
a gift to the Guru

   He is
wasting
away bone
by bone: cancer

eats at his
marrow for flight /we

are flesh
of Feeling-

I like
to remember his
smile

the way John told it

the night before they'd moved their bodies
together in love-fields whose ripe wheat
tingled rainbow sounds & so they hadn't minded
the blackout that closed the east. later,
they'd walked out under the stars, following deer
tracks uphill in the invulnerable night.
this, he said, defined their togetherness.
mary's long dress had picked up burrs, thorns,
moonlight and her face was the only star
he'd ever set his sights by. once at the crest
they'd heard a wildcat scream for love. they
laughed & smoked another joint of homegrown
kinnikinnick mixed with grass. then they had cried,
holding hands, feeling so small, so helpless
that they couldn't even think
about why someone had killed John F. Kennedy
or where Texas was at that moment wrenched from
time. the birches, he said, looked the same
as always. what felt menacing
was that nothing
had changed.

mary's testament

i tried,
no one can say
different
strokes applied.
my man john, whose book
is he starring in?,
expected i'd ask for out
when it was what he
wanted, can i say he was wrong?

i leave my womanlife
to my daughter
who ran away from home
to california, having
at sixteen enough faith
& coolth
to resurrect herself
houdinilike,
from the grave waters
of bitterness john & i
had rooted in
by our shared attitude
of hip indifference
to the nature of pain,
to ignorance.

i tried to heal
us all
& failed to recognize
you go directly to hell
when you avoid
—like racecar drivers
don't—fouled-up
sparkplugs, dirty
carbs, too low
a pressure
in tires that must roll
over corrugated
country roads.

i thought someone else
would take on being
the mechanic. when the
accelerator pedal jammed
i retired
my machine. john
stayed high
if you can call it that
when the heart clouds over
like a faulty t.v. screen.

i leave my love.
go on with my problems.

BRIGID MURNAGHAN

George Washington: A Dialogue Between Mother & Daughter

MAMA:
"In the name of God how
could he have won our
freedom?
He must have spent all
his time posing."

ANNIE:
"Maybe he gave the English
a picture of himself."

Daisy

Why don't you wear a daisy in
        your hair . . .
Instead of one of those hothouse flowers.

A daisy soon dies out of water
All the daisies in the city are
        hothouse anyway.

When I see daisies I want to see
        a field covered
So I can stretch out and know if
        they were picked they'd be
                dead in an hour.

Paint me a daisy to wear in my hair
If you're right it will have the
Look of my beautiful child!!!

Chinatown

once in chinatown
    there lived a lady
she wanted to be white
    she was a lousy cook

Mother's Day

once a mother
    always a mother
some get flowers
    others candy
but, if we train them well,
    we may get vodka . . .

Tweeds

the nice thing about them
is that you can
    live in them
    sleep in them
    even pee the bed in them
wake up the next morning
    wear them and have
people tell you how nice
    you look,
Just like a Lady!

For My Mother

Here I am
born of a second and
too many years of her daydreams
So many years she could not understand
     the joy of pain
nor understand that she was bringing
     the truth of her love into a cold world.

Could she not understand the pain
     I would have to suffer being
     her first born . . . a girl child.

As the wise old woman said to the king
     "Be your first born a girlchild
     she shall know the love of men
     But will search an eternity for
     the love of a mother."

The bridge of all bridges
The Brooklyn Bridge
How great it stands
On its man cut stone
What a shame it only goes to Brooklyn.

....

The smell of the fish market
City birds chasin' butterflies
In the name of progress they are rippin' us off again
The artists down there are puttin' up a fight to keep their homes
Now that the rich are being chased out of Soho by the tourist
Even the pigeons kiss in New York in the springtime
There is a song on the juke box
"A native New Yorker"
I love you New York because you make me feel so real
I love you New York because you're beautiful
I love you New York because you never bore me.

....

The fog in Washington Square Park is London fog
Where have you gone, Empire State Building?
Have they stolen you?
Where have you gone, Twin Towers?
Who'd steal you?
Why have you left me alone?
Why have you isolated me?
When will the wind come and blow the fog away
So I can see my lifelines once again.

First Asparagus of Spring

Danny kissed me in the kitchen
followin' me to the stove—
reassurin' me it was Spring.

Danny kissed me in the kitchen
tellin' me I was mortal.

Danny kissed me
showin' how easy it was
to throw me off.

Danny kissed me in the kitchen
reassurin' me it was Spring.

Dear sweet asparagus.
I shall not forsake thee
and run off.

But, Danny kissed me in the kitchen.

MARGARET RANDALL

Come Winter

come winter come us
in our longing come
hearing and touching and
being come over and

under the strangeness
and not to be precious
about it: what

growing what grasping what
grazing in marshes of
mournful illusion, the

wonder unhands us the
verses compile a
history's needing and

you the bearer and I
the bearer and we the
joining and we the halting
and we in abundance of

singing and screaming of
spilling in prelude to
passion and poison a

desolate dancing a
holocaust haunting the
range of our finding and

bearing our dreaming
to burn.

Ecstasy is a Number
(for Jack)

All is Number. Number is in all.
Number is in the individual.
Ecstasy is a Number.
    —Charles Baudelaire, *Squibs*

tremor tempo our
own voice and
catwalk descending
descended half-hypnotic
midday racing just
behind, half out-swung
and colorless, dizzy
metered limp balance
loose-knit of sense and
summer, wake of total
recall (there is endless
substance, soft soft)
stroking the brain-sharp
vision, stroking stroking
the brain, stroking from
pits of black laughter,
black laughter, idly playing
with the pieces (is it
still raining?) dying
in the light.

On Seeing an Old Man Die
in the Street

No sound so silent
As inhaled destiny
With none to follow
Down Sixth Avenue

Required ritual
The only ceremony
Momentary hesitation
Down Sixth Avenue

Life settling on
The pavement
Dry of tears
Down Sixth Avenue

And I keep walking
Past that moment
A heartbeat out of place
Down Sixth Avenue.

Any Little Boy
Wanting to be President

Any little boy wanting to be president?
Pogo stick dynamos, city parks of
crocodile tracks (despite him
no spik inglis velly well)
street stones to slingshot
to arrows to pistols to
one germ warfare in
every gum wrapper,
tanks, missiles,
atom bomb and
more—
Any little boy wanting to be president?
Him doesn't know and playing anyway,
ah, but him knowing it better than
we, us, our—sons and daughters
smoking the same pipes of sub-
mission and no mind the
freud and god and
endless academies
some little boys
coming up still
wanting to be
president in
spite of it
all!

St. Margaret Stepping from the Belly of the Dragon
(for Naomi)

(written with visions of the early Titian,
St. Margaret and the Dragon.
Prado Museum, Madrid, Spain)

St. Margaret stepping from the belly of the dragon
jumping dancing out-flung prayer book in hand and rosary
the beads a black line to the bottom of the painting
like the knotted intestines of bulls when they
make the sausage, the roman maiden full of faith dancing and
pushing the devil behind her like a wild cha-cha full of
faith and softness with a shining storming sky of Titian
splendor breathing deep heartbeats of wetness and the girl
again, ripe for a man, gleaming chastity her spawning skirt
sucked damp across her thighs with the dragon's steaming saliva

that roman maiden springing into a cement world with her
prayer book and rosary and wet thighs her warm wet
hair her white toes on the sweat cold stones it isn't
a prayer book and rosary after all but an empty cross a
stalwart stagnant cross. I don't care how far you've wandered
St. Margaret or how long or lost or where or when or how it feels
to be holy. We were made to dance St. Margaret and you knew it
and if you didn't you should have St. Margaret we were meant
to dance. We were meant to feel the wet cloth across our

thighs and love the feel of it hugging the soft spots, it
has to be more somehow to loose the humbleness and reach and
not in that way but reach out and touch it the different idea
moving as you find that it's there, knowing it all the time
but finding the knowing, feeling the gradations ochre and
glad. The world is not as it was St. Margaret you can breathe
a little now along the rim of the edge's edge. The thinking
comes later St. Margaret and you ride on a horse but you
hurry too much you hurry.

Untitled, Unnumbered

As you came, and
I, hoping it wouldn't be
or more than the wish dreams
of after—how does it
happen, with thoughts
constructed of training?
Give me or take, and
how to feel when
the mold is long made
and all the sense of it
known? The teaching
taking its own toll
in time's substance.
One should know the
words then, but
doesn't.

Number 5
(for Elaine)

Here we can listen
to nightfall
and blow in
the ears of
sunsets
while the
earth
staggers
through
an open
door.

Thelonius
(for Walter)

Monk played with
his hat on—rest
that hat man! spilled
the liquid voice and
his sound comes slow

slow the blind
sure joy ha the
ha ha wail hard the
off-time play cool
it man cool

cool wail of
the hot beat
heavyjuice air and
Monk played with
his hat on, but he
got plenty of hair!

Still Life with Ketchup

This is for he and she and the others, you
and all the kids back home, play it
again! But it's not like that
anymore. Was it ever?
Collages of faces.
Why are we here?
And why then?
Having it like pictures
unframed in winter, or
the other kind.

Sitting back. A dirty table
is as good as any other. The talking
goes on, and the dust trickling through
beer and the new year again and
again. One of it touches the other
in a different sort of light.

Still, the image is here. A poem
is as good, part of it means, part
of it does mean and you
touch it, too.

Of Our Time

it will be something
of our time, my
love

something of our time
you and the question
turned in on itself

angels too have a place
in the scheme of
things and

you speak of the ravages
of contentment: then
my thoughts: an

echo after the rape
of our senses, an
image remains.

Gesture

analyzing last remembered dream (already
        a week old) the taste of too much
smoke spewing the sense of it

as: did you make it, baby? asking because
        it didn't happen, dropping out
of sight between your touch

or, does it matter really outside desperation
        closing in while you stand bleak-
white against endless light

sounds of living (contact) drowned from
    the ear's need caressing empty minute

        pick it up   eat it

LAURA ULEWICZ

Pinpoint

—for A. G. and B. K. in memory of 1010

It came like light out of the walls,
Like sunny days, like judgment.
Like dusk when the light comes out of the road,
When sky is only there,
When under the earth is known,
Is known, but doesn't matter.
It came out of you, me, and out of the wall
Like not owning but loving,
Like not having to lock doors.
Like a light out of the sea it came
When seagulls lean revealed
Real in their color—
Grey and white as we say they are
And more:
Purple and private with private vision.

It was as if we could live exchanges of being
With egg cartons covering cracks in the wall
Through which the wind was blowing.
The wall, wall; and we, human.
Really so—no confusion,
No fear.
It came.
And I no longer wanted to be anything
But simple.
I thought, "We are dying,
And the wall is dying,
And it will never matter again
Because we are here now,
Really here,
Being."

Yes, that was the right obsession.

—1959

Written in recollection of the days before a movement got stopped by being named and publicized too soon. A. G., who stayed sane through fame, B. K., who changed radically through speed, and 1010 Montgomery which was torn down.—L. U.

Letter Three

Page one

Like these geraniums that sun
Rises to claim us, will not be ignored
As if the sea were within us,
And no ark anywhere.

Lie down, lie down, Geraniums.
So much continuous blossoming
Injures the eyes of the heart of the beast
Accustomed to transience.

And you, Beast, panicked by weariness,
Soothe yourself back to magnificence.
You who escaped with yourself from the ark
Need strength beyond that to create
Freedom in freedom.

Page two

Because there was no ark
Some little known beast of the sea
Learned water from waves, and rolled
Over the antique burden of itself.

Because there was no ark
Some delicate beast at bay
All common-seeming, met
The oncoming waves with hysteria.
Its most grotesque movement
Revealed some grace.

Because there was no ark
Some crafty beast of a dragon
Built intricate castles of shell
Wherein it moved with the grace of chiffon
The color of saffron.

Page three

Stand where you will and think of the whales:
How they'll not come ambling the Umbrian hills
or smile in your window, or nibble your grape leaves;
but tunnelling where they must to make their waves
and break their waves to patterns of grape leaves,
they will evade you, as the sea evades you.

When saying, "It is merely water," even
the most apt sea-maiden drowns, remember
their schools touring home through the sea.   Neither
rooted nor uprooted, unlike geraniums,
the whole sea is their ark.   Or else they are.

Yet variable orbited, placed,
they too will float their massive bellies up.
When your last whale has died, you'll still find left
this fierce deliberate sun which grows—from which
there is no ark, or no ark suitable—
till sun on the land and on the ocean, sun,
each summer day is a day of intolerable judgment.

Third Generation

"Daughter, Daughter, have ye brung me any gold,
Any gold fer to pay my fine?"
"No, I jest come fer to see you hanged,
Hanged from the gallows line."
          —American folk song.

I saw my father fishing in the lake
Delighting in the broken scales of fish
        As if he could forget himself, forget,
        As if he could forget himself in fish.

I saw my mother timid in her book.
To break my mother, father broke her book
        As if she could discover on some page
        That he could not discover life in life.

I saw my father eating cabbage soup
Five times a week, kielbasa, sour cream
        As if he fed a hidden root that grew
        Inside a Poland he had never seen.

I saw my mother getting her revenge,
A private crucifix behind her private door.
        As if by shedding skins they could unite
        Or get revenge for what would not unite.

I saw my father nailing amber boards
Because my mother's need became his pride
        As if they could forget themselves, forget
        In a house that now entombed them both.

I saw my mother pregnant in her sleep
Turn on the gas while walking in her sleep
        As if in sleep she still could not forget
        Though she forgot her days in sleep.

I saw my father hanging in my soul.
I'd lost those golden fish to pay his fine.
        As if I could forget my halves, forget
        I am the paradox, and must resolve them both.

Sargasso Sea

Sun begins to enter the lounge
Filled with puzzles and the sound of the sea.
Cool in the rhythm of fans and moon
She sits in her flesh in a lemon dress.
She is looking for a piece of the puzzle.

In a pattern of sun in a lemon dress
She waits for a thought to come
Like a man striding into the room.
It comes, on the Sargasso Sea,
Water like any other. It enters the lounge

Riddled with puzzles and the sound of guns.
Nothing to fill their time but heat
The sailors shoot the flying fish;
And the thought sits down inside her
Pleating its skirts like a nun.

Manhattan as a Japanese Print

In spring there are no skyscrapers.
Invisible flowers bloom between tall menaces.
Japanese glass mountains, maybe.
We crawl by mysteries inside.

I say there are no skyscrapers.
Only the travellers clustered
Paused on their journey.
At times the flowers. Turning a corner
We smell them, we almost see them;
Or the wind turns a corner. Abruptly
Flowers spring out of its bloodstream.

They cannot be picked anymore than the wind
Can be picked. Neither can time be picked,
Yet it is there. And how could the travellers know
It was time to be spring,
If there were no flowers,
If there were only skyscrapers?

Discover or build,
But give me no skyscrapers.
Give me the horse of the wind
That feeds on flowers.
I'd ride him discriminate, mountainously
To the source, to the feedbin.

No, there are no skyscrapers.
Neither is there a god of skyscrapers.
We move by mysteries inside invisible flowers.
Yet sometimes turning a corner,
Sometimes I've almost seen
That incalculable it
Scratching its back on stars.

And once I grew tired of turning corners
And stood sleep still.
But the earth kept turning my dreams around.
When I awoke I was not in the same place.
Face to face I stood with a skyscraper.

Celebration in Oregon

Halcyon, sing!
Kingfishers, kingfishers,
Flash out of willows
Over Columbia.

Twenty-eight kingfishers—
Halcyon, sing—
For twenty-eight rings
In the tree of my birth.

If Columbia grieves
She grieves without legend.
Halcyon, sing,
Interpret her waters.

Kingfishers, kingfishers,
Faster than rivers,
Perch in her reeds to hear
Halcyon sing.

bia rages
Aegean
hear
g.

y river,
Riotous water,
Obstinate blood,
Pride-swollen spinster!

Oriental those reeds
That marry her water—
Oh my white barked
Precarious alder.

And yet, when Columbia sings,
Kingfishers, kingfishers
Cover the limbs
Of my birthday.

Twenty-eight kingfishers—
Oh my pride—
Challenge her water,
Alive plummeting birds.

Aphrodite Declining

Devious Aphrodite's eyes,
Green as young olives,
Scanned her thighs—carefully plucked
And tawny as the oil of olives.
"Time," she said, "to quit
Playing Goddess of Love.
Time to find
What I am goddess of."

She looked askant her eager hip and eyed
A distant silky-skinned pale fellow
Who beckoned listlessly and flicked
His delicate hair into the wind.
So many boys, she learned, like Paris

Want to make use of a goddess
For gain or practice.

Spurious Aphrodite
Found herself amused
By a Macedonian painter:
"A perfect combination
Of intellect and satyr."
He threw away his paints
Having found his muse;
She threw away the painter,
Claimed herself abused.

Curious Aphrodite peeked
Over the edge of her precipice,
Spotted in that feminine abyss
A masculine wonder,
Swaggering thunder
And thighs all furry.
She slid in a flurry of growls and groans
And clutched at him to save
The marrow of her bones.

Furious Aphrodite, middle aged and wise,
Glared at her mate and 7 children
With olive and pimento eyes.
Intent on giving birth to her true nature
She leapt in a fury
Of nail and tongue
Upon the unsuspecting satyr.
(Later when arraigned in the high court
She blamed Zeus
And the children for it.)

But time kept growing up
And Greece fell down.
A serious Aphrodite left for Rome,
Moved more by night,
Preferred a sheerer gown,
And busy with affairs
Now lived alone.
They said for Caesar's love
She changed her name—

Not for the love of the man
But for his crown.
Otherwise, they said, she stayed the same.

Querulous Aphrodite sneaked
One wistful mirror-look
Into her pit of olive eyes,
Then suddenly, to all antiquity's surprise,
She wrote a book
Denouncing plucking thighs.
She planned to be Pliny's polemic bride,
But she caught Christianity and died.

McNichols Road, 1951

It is a long time since I confused my
childish shrinking from other people's
pain with the strong and gentle pity
of the saints.
                    —Bernanos, *Diary of a Country Priest*

Apples, luggage, and a cleft palate. Hot-clutched
Tiger Lilies wilting. With her split lip,
Her dog-child brain, with her hair pathetically prettied,
She waits at my same bus stop, and will not stop
Talking. All she has to say is the way she can
Say it. My will, polite, withdraws me. But the soul
Of my body is ashamed at the way my mind's affronted.
I am in hot schism. While she, so stunted to the core
Of her being, she guesses me out. The more obvious freaks
Have always snuffled me out. I am doomed to listen.
They sit on the arm of my chair as I read the paper,
Demand their share of the real communion I withhold.
They swarm in dreams with insects I have swatted,
Halved by accident, allowed to drown.
Ach, how I hate them when they drag their King
On center. Yet how he conjures pity, commands
Pity. King of maniacs, of morons
King of lechers, King of worms. At first

They only jab at him with crutches. Then they
Sting his eyes out, decide to leave his tongue
Because they like hearing how they mean no harm.
They castrate him, of course. They suck his blood
Whining meanwhile for understanding which he
Gives—for they refuse it each other—until
I too despise him. Though I will never join them
Or be his queen, whenever they come to me one
By one, I am doomed to listen. Partly from fear.
Because they have right to claim me as one of their own.

Te Deum

Here on this braided rug I bought and tend,
that I borrow from Your decay,
among these cats, those sirens,
I kneel here where it is still Your field
In praise of You,
Your lust still on me, hearty appetite,
my body too much alone.

Here on this rug, my spirit reaching up
through the red ceiling to Your stars,
I am of these cats, Your cats, I am of Your stars.
Now I am braided over and under Your being—
part of this rug, which is earth,
I am ready.
prepared for Your death which is change,
which is moving from union toward union,
prepared,
and You let me live on . . .

poem to your lean face, leaning down eyes
How you know
    with length by heart & depth by fingers
stretching
       to reach me.

Down undercover where the heart pulls no
     word needs speaking
Enough to hear the call through a horn played
                 beyond mechanics.

probing, no one can unearth the cache
    hidden, giving itself away.

I remember the first time New York overwhelming drear
tenements, halfweathers of sky-tattered phantoms,
Starcrossings only at corners: the Encroachment
graved in my palm,
             for remembering;
A haven of weatherblown pigeons
unfriendly with corn—
& my mother led me round corners, we
rollerskating backwards veered off from
the slightest calamity;
O impaled privacy! City beckoning/ I
came & built the wall spherical pyramid
Cheops' canoe & enclosed myself. Carefully
the shell slid onto the current bearing
me, safe against frailty (but
    crossing no visible waters hearing
    no sun streaming seeing
    no fish in the water:
Blind glyph on the testament seas!

      til at last
it was done
& fell, all of it,
      down
& was open.

& whoever approached, entered in, & left
        leaving a gaze in the air.
Until you
        where the streak of lightning left
                indelibly its imprint
came
& cleaved to
                (with length of heartstring & fingers
reaching)
                (the glowing coals, the firmament's touchstone
O Vast narrowed into the map of your face!

O love pure love in the universe
    pierce me and pour in
that I live outside the wall
the flourish of wilderness grasses
High—& see not that
familiar circle of leaves
to step back to.

                                                65–66.

thrumming with it Lord thrumming with it
life is the magic machine still
pulling itself through swamps brown with
      crocodiles and a heavy sun
the mud and sinking of it—even this
thrumming
            and somewhere slowly coming, a gladness
        in back of the magic machine
is thrumming

the cliché of it, waiting for death
yet open to life
      half-closed in death,
the ocean getting warmer in the sun.
the ocean, and there is no end to mysteries;
and the catchstone of treasures hidden under the stars
til the eyes are opened, dazzled at the seeing.

millions of deaths I walk through
      pulling the empty air
millions of deaths of all his faces &
      death is grown no fatter
a million faces medium rare & death
      is still hungry, getting thinner.

threatening, cajoling, welcoming, inviting—
I have played with the thin man
      tempting no one but myself.

                                    ny/ 6–66.

Poem Against Endless Mass Poetry Readings

O the tyranny of assembled poets
    beleaguering ears & the shoulder muscles
the blade cracks in my jaw & the
                    head pangs.
Heavy underhanded deviousness
    herding us in
        & cramming us with it—

O the long thin arms & barrel clustered ears!

full hours it takes me unwinding
/stark hands on the tablecloth twitching,
    & drinking even as I would not otherwise
        /unnerved & pallid

O pay yr dues before ye lord it over

    me,
        Poets!
in silence/ the angels are breathing.

san francisco/ spring 67

to Ray:

Junk (& the old man) Changes

   the camps divided
   & lines drawn taut

I am subsided back to a true regard
  (taken advantage of:
   genius of tyranny)

—abjectness of lethargy & its
  self-contempt:
Let me sleep & pass over abysses & lone places
  Please.

water hums in a desolate bathroom
& the walls drum magnified pertrified silence
logging the eardrums with solitude
desolate & self-examining/ let not the thought be
      swayed by teary despair
from penetration to the core & kernel of it—
  trust or untrust . . . ?

the heart may be a lonesome animal
   but not crippled, &
feeble the will: not entirely inert

face to it/ barely/
   & be glad

that the eye see clearly & be done with deception

/there is no reason otherwise to stay
   prone & weeping

& self deceit is a house fallen down.

Take care the time passed over
   leaving the withered soul unlaughing
    be not forgotten or left unlearned/
throw loose the maniacal guilt &
   bondage of caution

tho every flick of the wrist be criticized
shall the soul die

or only bleed the more, to be
free of the nameless thing there
     lodged in the bloodstream
          dejecting the spirit,
               inheriting doom as its portion?

no mock profile of courage, this
nor feary knees in the unknown waters/

One simple straight & inner truth:

     respect for another soul in its
               preciousness also
     respect for your own.
     oncoming catastrophe
     impressing its ramifications in the
                         iron sky
Chatter not so, all the possible sunderings
/hold to the soul he has given thee
turning not left nor to right
     but in deeper;
Submerged, the lungs learn to take in more air
& wax elastic at the last.

fillmore sf./ summer '67.

Poem/Exhortation

1. out riding
majestic, the landscape passing
this world of the eyes
                    /sweetened
by seeds of the fields.

flickering forest leaf shadows passed
     down into depths of sleep
          imprinted.
(everything the eyes have seen
          imprinted.
          EVERYTHING.
everything, everything, everything, everything, everything,

everything, everything.

—near to the brink of the mouth,
crowding immense at the thin shell,
Waiting to break thru/ spill out the soul
                              from its pocket
free.
into thousandfold manifest wonders:
A Oneness/ over all the mind knows
                                    /
                         knowing but a portion.

(uncertainties in the serious life . . .? . . .
—O backyard flatland greenhouse
     town in the lowland
          sheltered & squinting

fear and trembling
     the only halt to natural progression
(. . . Ah sentience of herb/
          the power prophesying
               possible life . . .

the fields are blessing the trees
     are blessing the forests and flowers
          blessing.
Lull of the fruits in the fields
                         /first seeding.

a tranquility contemplates
     its centre
     . . . hovering . . .

One month before mid-summer's night
     & already the land is yielding.
          in the fullness of air: Behold/
               I AM.

Van Gogh's spring apple orchard
     & the windy Stonehenge
met and mingled.

     there is a prayer of hands
     the earth is dancing
up onto its feet/out over the floor

—cows in the yellow field wooden bridge stream
                    /dimly moving
Dream visions of ULTIMATE GRASS.

Impossible world, Ray Bremser
    wielding the intricate knife
        carving the intimate vision.

the foothills mammoth greenbearded feet
stepping down to the water—
    /ancient lowering down to drink
inherent in herbs and grasses. . . .

        tall fields
        of grasses.

expanse of water
        touching the knees of the hills.
Stork legs sticking up under houses
        perched
                out on the eaves of Stream.

the Lay of the Land, heaping
            hills and far valleys.

blessed & apportioned
the earth sown, increases.

inherent blossoms
    emblazon the moment flown
this silent portion of eternity
        Rising.
How Much I Love Your Creation!
    How much I love it!

the crowned & tallest
Redwood, springing/ dark
bread of the bark against green.

—pressure of the toe bearing down in the
    footprint/ Spell of
night winging waters
    curtailing of Mind-Blown from
all the apparent blossoming/
    cut short & leaned over. . . .

looking down into the slants and rises
for the lost soul
    Remember the light.
        O do not go wandering.

the growing open/ in any age
    leaps back
        to the brink:
all the ages of wonder are equal.

with every breath is the body's age grown down
    upon it/ the heartbeat sandglass certainty
        of wearing away;
yet the mind drifts back to the Wonder:
    What more? What less? What else is there, ever?
to eyes, bright with vision
    comes apparent the blossoming.

2. *come home*

the curlicues & rust of mossagate
    worded into tomes,
the elemental voice intaling,
    hear it!

the guardian angel
    alights in a darkened corner
        flourishing arrows
to pierce the thin thing thru
& ring me down chimes.

speak of me who sits in a withered stone/ castle vault/
    muttering running commentary

in powers audible and still/
    playing over the mechanism like a piano;
the human body interred & animated,
      O Divine & Limping Puppet
                in eternity
the gears are grinding/ the soul passes fluttering
    under the bridge/
        out into the Light/ ecstatically bursting!
      All the particles cling to the Host
        & Vessel of Brightness.

(the tomb of the dead is swept clear of lingering)
from the realm of shadows is the angel
come home.

marin county, cal 5/67

ANNE WALDMAN

After "Les Fleurs"
—Paul Eluard

I am 20 years old and holding on
Knowing I'm still young, I love you world

I am not 20 years old. My past is deaf, deaf

I dream a life of crystals and lie down in the grass

You think I'm crying; I don't
Don't hurt me—let me be

My eyes a strength the color of my wounds,
Love, what is the sun when it rains?

I tell you there are things as true as this story

When I close my eyes I kill you.

College Under Water

Who are these women and offices
that control the will of the dead graduates?

They come to dinner like swimmers
assembling before a final race

Now coffins are lined up outside
where campus elms seize precedence over girls

Now offices are closed for the afternoon
in correspondence with the courts and the pool

Now because instructed the sky changes hands
shuffling wills that are transferred

to file cards behind locked doors
These vendetta women will not be put off

Now I write like this because
it could happen   My will weakens

Is there a choice? the alternative
lies on the other side of the poem.

The Blue That Reminds Me
of the Boat When She Left

Folds on your shirt lie like shadows
who hide me before she's leaving
You know she's leaving. The flag signals
us to mask and cross a plank so that
the transition will be easier, less visual
The sun has moved a bit and
sadness takes on new shapes
You say "Her shape sleeps in me and
the world explodes around her until
every atom resembles the match trick
she taught us last night"
We translated the dream before she left
then waited in the park by the dock
under shadows that were increasing
on your shirt as the sun grew feeble
Now she sends us postcards of sky & sea that say:
"I have had crazy dreams lately! Last night
I was dead and my skin was the color of this picture."

The De Carlo Lots

1

You are parceled out over the post office
Letters arrive from Jonathan, Sasha
A season in Millville, New Jersey.

The voice is feedback and not insensitive
to moths as light   dispersed in spots

through this room. When I see the particles
who rations these waves for me?

Only that you might sit here unafraid
listening to the termites eat out the walls
and wonder how they do it   the stamina,
I mean the breeding

It was about the family he confided.
The effect this might have on them
could not be ignored, even as they slept

And when letters would arrive the next morning
after the bicycle, who was to say
where was her heart in all of this?

2

Mailbags under the porch.
A calm across the lake.

The family hurts me as I lounge about
these pine walls trying to read
A scratching in the wood prevents sobriety, or else
the knowledge of it ending with the itching never
subsided.

The letters are damp with use.
My fingers are moist.
Inkstains cover the tablecloth
that now resembles "black"

A song that will always have the same hold
on you is painful for me, you see, because
I never even knew it and have nothing to
counter your passion,   the energy
with which you embrace the other girl's radio

3

She is no longer of use to them
when they forsake the lake for the ocean

In fact, she's almost a hindrance, the
way she likes to "cut-up" everything,
keeps using up paper   writes letters

and they don't let her go anyway
All the way.

You're swimming nude in the ocean.
It's 2:00 AM. Some policemen will come
and ask you to go   gently
when they see how young you are

You will mount the stairs to the attic
of the house where you're staying
the "house of Lynn's aunt who is away,"
and you will be surprised to see her
there between two beds,   two boys
They are putting on their clothes when
she says no,   don't go

Dear Jon,   This is Atlantic City
I am thirteen years old   This is the
birthday of the song they're playing
when they interrupt us eight years later

4

We are saying goodbye to the inanimate objects.
They are mostly of wood.
Light seeps through these cracks,
as squirrels in winter
when the lady comes cleaning up
misses them under the bedsheets

I am trying to imagine the light in winter, not
being told   as squirrels, termites.
I am learning how they live from books.
We are writing "Ten Facts" in the city.

Light defines these cracks which are of wood
as you are "my only shape and substance"
or the voice is dispersed in outlines
of spots through the room.

A beam crashes the dials.
I am thinking now of all the little animals.

5

The family is livening up the house
with the radio   but she is not there
and is only told later
the pine was "rocking"

You are perhaps on a boat watching
the children watching the sunset from the pier
or else fishing by the sand-bar, adoring the heron
The boat is rocking.

She is rationing out her love, as waves
are sectioned out over the lake
disappearing into the land,
sending the energy home

She remembers the couple going over the dam
in the canoe. Strangers from Vineland, New Jersey.
A song attached to them immediately.

These are foreign waters foreign objects float upon.
They are large splinters of wood and resemble
the pieces of letters
I can't seem to get off to you, off the shore

6

The bicycle trip is arduous and not unlike
the energy it takes descending these steps daily
seeing if the mail has come at 9:30 AM.

The energy is parceled out into the day.
His legs are weak from making love.

The forces it takes licking the envelope in
Athens come at me as the sounds shaking
the foundations of the house they're tearing apart.
It is of pine.
Only the land is not yours   the rest you may carry away,
while a telephone number tells you all the particles

Sasha's letter is brief.
He tells me he is happier in the water than
any other place and hopes to live there forever.
A couple crashes over the dam a splinter away.

7

We are dwelling on the surface of
something explosive, though not unlikely
subdued
as the cracks are blocked up with tissue.
Light or fire. It's all the same to me.

Where were they going from the post office
when she asked, are you driving back?
From Atlantic City where the music is live
and we turn on the radio   trying to capture
those lost waves

A naked girl is swimming in her view.
I've come here year after year.
The family hurts me as I try to swim,
abandoning these walls of pine and
what they represent in terms of "destructibility"

All my friends are entering the lake for the last time
as the energy leaves my birthplace and returns
to the city in September.
We study leaves, the lifespan of termites.

A great blast splinters the shelf that
holds the radio   when the voice
reaches me a second away and embraces
the girl fishing from the rowboat.

The sun is setting across the shore.
This is about the family who lived there.

I write to Jonathan and Sasha about the fireworks,
as the last song is rationed into the night

8

The dials are lots and are as inanimate
as the ground we walk on
That is to say, not without life or
waverings in the soil

He was as young as the girls who surrounded
him and they used to watch him mounting the
attic steps, going,   as he said,   to pray

Outside, a calm across the lake.
A peace after the accident.
A break in the day where "demolition"
ruled their lives,
gradually governed their words   their sleep
as she worried about the effect
this might have on all of them.

She would never let the others touch him
or played the radio when he came.
He told her she had cut herself up in little pieces
equally rationed among them and might easily
go away and never return,
only referring to the songs to counter
the energy of the other girl's swimming or
recall the light seeping through the cracks.

He said "I am thirteen years old"
That was eight years ago, when the dials
spilled all over the page

9

You are allotted a childhood as wood
splinters right under your thumbs.

It's as quickly as that, seeing the
children put on their clothes again
asking you not to turn away, but
to look back upon the waves again,
to even touch their burning limbs

Letters will record this season even
if the radio doesn't

And the wood eats the dials right
out of the pine

I mean the stamina with which this
whole life span is devoured

The family forgets.
The girl rises from the water and
comes towards us on the shore.

I am picking up the pieces to send to you,
measuring the lots, the dreams by

1966

How the Sestina (Yawn) Works

I opened this poem with a yawn
thinking how tired I am of revolution
the way it's presented on television
isn't exactly poetry
You could use some more methedrine
if you ask me personally

People should be treated personally
there's another yawn
here's some more methedrine
Thanks! Now about this revolution
What do you think? What is poetry?
Is it like television?

Now I get up and turn off the television
Whew! It was getting to me personally
I think it is like poetry
Yawn   it's 4 AM yawn   yawn
This new record is one big revolution
if you were listening you'd understand methedrine

isn't the greatest drug no not methedrine
it's no fun for watching television
You want to jump up have a revolution
about something that affects you personally
When you're busy and involved you never yawn
it's more like feeling, like energy, like poetry

I really like to write poetry
it's more fun than grass, acid, THC, methedrine
If I can't write I start to yawn
and it's time to sit back, watch television
see what's happening to me personally:
war, strike, starvation, revolution

This is a sample of my own revolution
taking the easy way out of poetry
I want it to hit you all personally
like a shot of extra-strong methedrine
so you'll become your own television
Become your own yawn!

O giant yawn, violent revolution
silent television, beautiful poetry
most deadly methedrine
                    I choose all of you for my poem personally

ruth weiss

from *THE BRINK*

just now afternoon
and the barren hills
brown with sun on them
had nooks & nooks of new
just getting to be grass
and zz sat on the rock out of the sun
take me away
before we come back here
and he pulled on the pullover
and curved the beach like bay
like yelapa
like anyplace in the world of heaven

LEAVE PARADISE

at the waterfall
falling the waters

the tadpole has brothers
does not know it
to live in paradise
is more difficult than not
to have thought it
to leave paradise
leave the thought of it
to enter
one must leave paradise

to clean water use earth
to clean earth use fire
to clean fire use air
to clean air
enter

all the ferns are jungle
the original leaf
it was huge once

is still bigger than most
and palm & evergreen
are shaking finger-tips

how do you do?
how do you do what?
i've just come from europe
where they learn english
the hard way

oh channel me to a funnel
and make me strong
islands can control
could in the past
if the sea was with
or enough against

TO BE RIGHT
IS THE MOST TERRIFICAL PERSONAL STATE
THAT NOBODY IS INTERESTED IN

he paints dark paintings in america

and the dark caves
were rocks with red fungi
fungus   omnibus
leaves
then oh sun sun sun
warm salt to sink in

see the up-arrow
follow it down
he found it
he buried it
LAUA VABO AVE
simple civilized essence
beyond

sand tastes good
like a beach should
tide coming
beyond

below is wet water
and barrels bobbin'

no fresh meat this week
open another can
and watch for any fires
or smoke or chart all plane
unknowns
may cross up there
your vision as good as any
your sight your knowing
it's all a moment how you cross
beyond

the brush & brush & stream
recorded it
beyond

they were here again
where the big tree
was not the
dream

and he said
she was right right
but wouldn't wait
she wouldn't

they jump jump by the sea
they wait
for the dangers to come in

you're a hard one
to head on to
and he built his house of wood
with one plank
PLUNK
plunk plunk by the sea
paddle broken water-line
the wind splintering
the beached boat

i am the begin
said the water
i was before you
said sand
and the shells rubbed screaming
against each other

you're a silly little sparrow
said one without wings

when they unbound a woman's feet
she strode ahead

it was such a quiet dinner
and at the awkward end
the magic hat again
only it was black
this time
and felt
and ageless & shapeless
and anyone who wore it
became many things
continually
beyond

back to the burning-pole begin
poor soul
he has a magic hat
he must dance
and she said fire-water
and would not dance with him
but whipped the word
the wind blew out the fire
and lights & lights & bay
recorded it
beyond

it was the last supper
once more
and they were eating
their small selves
continually
and the gate was locked
in the bright afternoon
by official notice
and the last supper
smoked to burning

and they played the game
he & she
the clown with no instrument

but hand & voice
beyond

the won ton woman
carried the hot dish across town
under her cloak
to keep it hot
instead of flying or sent for
her neighbor she was sick

wanton woman
where were you at the supper?

i want my man

and he said why talk
we'll only confuse
and she said it's much nicer
that way
and he laughed under his hat
to keep from crying

beyond the door & steps
they met again
and he moved her belongings
to his table
while she went to the ladies
and returning sat at her belongings
where they were moved
the same waiter at this table
so the confusion was easy

he told about his grandmother
and picnics
on the bus & weaving
it was the sun & high
and the bus lurched too
the shopping ladies sat grim
and then they too laughed
they too remembered
grandmother picnic
in the lurching sun

beyond the last stop
is the sea

over the balcony again
the ship mess
and the door had portholes
to round that illusion
yes he said
i cry not for me
but for them
whose crying i throw into my paintings
to throw back to them
and they do not see their crying

merry-go-round by the sea
the goats wore roses
the lions wore frogs
the black horses monkeys
the white horses angels
the brown ones with devils
and serpents with griffins

the clown said
i send messages from hell
that's why they run
is paradise hell
the way through?
there's a way of heaven
when hope is gone
there's a way of hope
when heaven is no more

start guessing
the clown again
give my love to the game
though i can't belong
the sun blinking
can make remember the night
the night is forgetting
remember the sea
and she asked again
where were you?
on a limb
limbo limbo lady-bug
all trees start with the first seed

BIOGRAPHIES

Mimi Albert (1940 –) was born in Brooklyn and raised in New York City, Mimi Albert came of age during the last years of the Beat Generation. She's published two novels about the era's effect on young women: *The Second Story Man* (Fiction Collective, 1975) and *Skirts* (Baskerville, 1994). She has also published fiction and nonfiction in anthologies and magazines in Europe and throughout the U.S., and won a number of grants and awards including the PEN NEA Syndicated Fiction award, a PEN USA grant, three California Arts Council grants, a New York State Council on the Arts grant, and a Yaddo Foundation grant. She currently lives in California, teaching in the U. C. Berkeley Extension writing program and at Napa State Hospital (for the mentally ill), as well as helping to coordinate the Napa Valley Writers' Conference. She is at work on a new novel set in Russia just before the Bolshevik revolution.

Carol Bergé (1928 –) was born on October 4th in New York City. She was anthologized in *Four Young Lady Poets* (Totem/Corinth, 1962), *The East Side Scene* (University of Buffalo Press, 1968), and *Seventh Street: An Anthology from Le Deux Megots* (Herperidian Press, 1961), among others. A prolific fiction writer, editor, and poet, she was editor/publisher of *CENTER* magazine and Center Press from 1970–83, and has taught at more than ten universities around the country and at many writers' conferences. Her books include: *From A Soft Angle: Poems About Women* (Bobbs-Merrill, 1971), *A Couple Called Moebius* (Bobbs-Merrill, 1972), *Acts of Love* (Bobbs-Merrill, 1973), *Fierce Metronome* (Window Editions, 1981), *Secrets, Gossip & Slander* (Reed & Cannon, 1983), and *Zebras: Or, Contour Lines* (Tribal Ctr. Press, 1991). Carol has put together an anthology entitled *Light Years: The NYC Coffeehouse Poets of the 1960s*, which is in search of a print publisher. She currently lives in Santa Fe, New Mexico, where she has owned and operated the Blue Gate Gallery of Art and Antiques since 1988.

Carolyn Cassady (1923 –) was born Carolyn Elizabeth Robinson on April 28th in East Lansing, Michigan. A distant relative of Sir Walter Scott, she graduated from Bennington after World War II. She earned an M.A. in fine arts and theater arts from the University of Denver. There she met Neal Cassady, Jack Kerouac, and Allen Ginsberg. In 1948 she married Neal; they had three children together, Cathleen, Jami, and John Allen (named after Jack Kerouac and Allen Ginsberg). She now lives in London, where she writes and paints.

Her reminiscences of her life with Neal and Jack were first published in *Rolling Stone* and the book *Heart Beat: My Life with Jack & Neal* (Creative Arts, 1976). Hollywood made a film version of the book which appeared in 1980. *Off the Road: My Years with Cassady, Kerouac, and Ginsberg* (Morrow, 1990) was a much expanded account of those years.

Elise Cowen (1933–62) was a classmate of Joyce Johnson's at Barnard College in 1950 and a major figure in Johnson's *Minor Characters* and also in her first novel, *Come and Join the Dance*. (Cowen also turns up in Irving Rosenthal's *Sheeper* and Herbert Huncke's *The Evening Sun Turned Crimson*, as well as in Huncke's autobiography, *Guilty of Everything*.) A tortured spirit, she was Allen Ginsberg's lover for a time in 1953, and after years in and out of institutions, finally jumped from the window of her parents' living room in Washington Heights on a February night in 1962. Many of her poems were destroyed by her parents after her death. Poems, gathered from her notebooks, were printed in *City Lights Journal* after her suicide.

Diane di Prima (1934 –) was born on August 6th in New York City. The granddaughter of Italian immigrants, she dropped out of Swarthmore College to become a writer. Her first poetry collection, *This Kind of Bird Flies Backwards* (Totem Press, 1958) was published by Hettie and LeRoi Jones. Her other books include: *Memoirs of a Beatnik* (Olympia Press, 1969), *Pieces of a Song: Selected Poems* (City Lights, 1990), *Seminary Poems* (Floating Island, 1991), *The New Handbook of Heaven* (Auerhahn Press, 1963), *Dinners and Nightmares* (Corinth Books, 1961), *Revolutionary Letters* (City Lights, 1971), and *Loba: Parts I–VIII* (Wingbow Press, 1978). Di Prima, the mother of five children, helped establish the Masters Program in Poetics at New College in San Francisco in 1980, and has worked privately as a psychic and healer.

Brenda Frazer (1939 –) was born in Washington, DC. She was the daughter of a State Department official and attended Sweet Briar College. She is best known for her memoir, *Troia: Mexican Memoirs* (Tompkins Press, 1969) written as Bonnie Bremser. (Published in London as *For Love of Ray* in 1971.) The book, volume two in a trilogy, is an autobiographical take on the difficult first five years of her marriage to the poet Ray Bremser, whom she married in 1959, and followed to Mexico in 1960 when he attempted to evade prison. The excerpt in this anthology is from the first volume of the trilogy, *Troia: Beat Chronicles*. She lives in Michigan.

Sandra Hochman (1936 –) was born on September 11th in New York and educated at Bennington. She is a poet, screenwriter, novelist, and playwright, and has written fiction for children. She won the Yale Younger Poets Award in

1963 for *Manhattan Pastures*. Other books include *Voyage Home*, *The Vaudeville Marriage*, *Love Letters from Asia*, *Earthworks: Selected Poems 1960–1970*, as well as the novels *Jogging*, *Walking Papers*, and *Playing Taho*. She lives and works in New York City.

Joyce Johnson (1935 –) was born Joyce Glassman on September 27th in New York City. Her *Minor Characters* (H. Mifflin, 1983) won the National Book Critics Circle award in 1984. Her novels include *Come and Join the Dance*, *Bad Connections*, and *In the Night Cafe*. She was a classmate of Elise Cowen's at Barnard College in 1950. She's worked most of her life in publishing, with editorial stints at William Morrow, the Dial Press, McGraw Hill, and Atlantic Monthly Press between 1965–86. Since then she has been a contributing editor to *Vanity Fair*, and has taught creative writing at the Bread Loaf Writer's Conference.

Kay Johnson (?) has seemingly disappeared off the face of the earth. She was a poet and artist who often published as Kaja. Her work appeared in *The Outsider*, *Residu*, *Olympia*, and *The Journal for the Protection of All Beings*. Her books include *Human Songs* (City Lights, 1964). She lived for a time in the Beat Hotel in Paris, and was featured in an article on the place in the December 1962 issue of *Town* with William S. Burroughs, Brion Gysin, and Harold Norse. She also appears in Harold Chapman's *The Beat Hotel*. Last anybody heard she was living in Greece.

Hettie Jones (1934 –) was born on July 16th in Brooklyn, New York, and is another of the "minor characters" in Joyce Johnson's Greenwich Village memoir. She went to the University of Virginia and Columbia University. She was the wife of the African-American writer LeRoi Jones and mother of their two daughters. Her memoir, *How I Became Hettie Jones* (Viking Penguin, 1990) traces her own journey as Hettie Cohen from Queens, to the wife of a radical poet and publisher of *Yugen* and Totem Press. She was managing editor of the *Partisan Review* from 1957–61. Her poetry and short stories have appeared in the *Village Voice* and elsewhere. Her award-winning books for children and young adults include *The Trees Stand Shinning: Poetry of the North American Indians* and *Big Star Fallin' Mama: Five Women in Black Music*. She lives in New York City.

Lenore Kandel (1932 –) was born in New York City of Turkish and Russian heritage. She moved to Hollywood because her father was a screenwriter and became something of a juvenile delinquent. She attended Los Angeles City College and the New School for Social Research in New York City. She was involved with the poet Lew Welch and Kerouac immortalized her as "Ramona

Schwartz" in his novel *Big Sur*. Her books and chapbooks include *An Exquisite Navel*, *A Passing Dragon*, and *A Passing Dragon Seen Again* (all Three Penny Press, all 1959), *The Love Book* (Stolen Paper Editions, 1966) for which she became infamous after the San Francisco police seized it as pornography in 1966, and *Word Alchemy* (Grove Press, 1967). She's still living in San Francisco.

Eileen Kaufman (1922 –) was born in Florida, taken to Minnesota at six weeks, stricken with pneumonia, and began a search for warmer country. During 1943–45 she served as a Wave in the U.S. Navy, in order to go to college on the G. I. Bill. She majored in English, minoring in Music, and continued her studies at UCLA and the Los Angeles Conservatory of Music. She sang in eight operas—both at the Wilshire-Ebell Theatre and the Hollywood Bowl, while getting her feet wet in advertising. In the 1950s she met Bob Kaufman, poet. It was overwhelming, and she moved to North Beach, married him the first time in Mexico—then to "Keep the Faith," married him at Bolinas Ridge atop Mt. Tamalpais in 1976. She became his archivist for the rest of her life, and cared for their son, Parker, before and after Bob's demise. Her life is documented in two books—*Beat Angel* and *Beat Vision*. The archives for Bob are in the Sorbonne, Paris, and Boston University's Mugar Museum.

Frankie "Edie" Kerouac-Parker (1923–1993) was dating Kerouac's pal Henri Cru when they were first introduced in 1940. She later married Jack Kerouac (who called her from jail to say he'd marry her if she'd post his bond) on August 22nd 1944. He lived with her and her parents in Grosse Pointe, Michigan, for a month, then worked briefly as a seaman. When they reunited in December 1944, they lived together in his room on the Columbia University campus, then moved into an apartment on 115th Street with Edie's old roommate Joan Vollmer Adams. By the time William Burroughs married Joan Vollmer in mid-January 1945, Edie had returned to Grosse Pointe for good. An excerpt from her memoir, *You'll Be Okay*, was published by Ridgeway Press in 1987.

Jan Kerouac (1952–96) was born Janet Michelle Kerouac on February 16th in Albany, New York. She was the daughter of Jack Kerouac and his second wife, Joan Haverty, but her father refused to acknowledge her as his offspring. She met Jack Kerouac for the first time in 1962, while getting a blood test to ensure child support, and only saw him one other time before his death. Her books are *Baby Driver* (St. Martin's, 1981) and *Trainsong* (Henry Holt, 1988). At the time of her death, she was working on *Parrot Fever*, about her mother.

Joan Haverty Kerouac (1931–90) met Bill Cannastra in Provincetown in 1949 and followed him to Manhattan. She didn't meet Jack Kerouac until after Bill's death and she and Jack were married just a few days later on November 17th,

1950. The marriage fell apart in July 1951, after Joan discovered she was pregnant with Jack's daughter Jan. Her unpublished memoirs, *Nobody's Wife*, cover the years 1949 to 1951. After her death, her children went through the house and discovered pages of the manuscript hidden about the house, even behind the walls. "The Wedding Chapter" was published as a chapbook in an edition of 240 copies for the Beat Generation conference at NYU, in May of 1994.

Joanne Kyger (1934 –) was born Joanne Elizabeth Kyger on November 19th in Vallejo, California. Her father was a career naval officer and her mother was from Saskatoon, Canada. She attended the University of California at Santa Barbara and in 1957 moved to North Beach in San Francisco. She was married to the poet Gary Snyder from 1960–64. Her books include *Going On: Selected Poems 1958–1980* (Dutton, 1983), *Just Space: Poems 1979–1989* (Black Sparrow, 1991), *The Japan and India Journals 1960–64* (Tombouctou Books, 1981), *Mexico Blonde* (Evergreen Press, 1981), and *Up My Coast* (Floating Island, 1981). She has taught at the New College of California in San Francisco and in the Poetics Program at Naropa Institute in Boulder, Colorado. She has lived in Bolinas, California, since the late sixties.

Fran Landesman (1927 –) was born Frances Deitsch on October 21st in Manhattan to a Seventh Avenue dress manufacturer and a former newspaperwoman. She attended Temple University and studied textile design at the Fashion Institute of Technology before running into Jay Landesman, editor of *Neurotica* in Greenwich Village. They gravitated to St. Louis where Fran wrote lyrics to Jay's musical productions: *The Nervous Set* (which played Broadway in 1959) and *Molly Darling*. The couple transplanted permanently to London in the spring of 1964. Fran's books include *The Ballad of the Sad Young Men* (Polytantric Press, 1975), *Invade My Privacy* (Cape, 1978), *More Truth Than Poetry* (The Permanent Press, 1979), *Is It Overcrowded in Heaven?* (Golden Handshake, 1981), *The Thorny Side of Love* (sun tavern fields, 1992), and *Rhymes at Midnight* (Golden Handshake, 1996). Fran is a frequent broadcaster on BBC radio and had a musical, *Did We Have Any Fun?*, with music by Simon Wallace, performed in London in the spring of 1996.

Sheri Martinelli (?) was an artist who ran into Diane di Prima in 1955, while Diane was in Washington, DC visiting Ezra Pound at St. Elizabeth's Hospital. Di Prima published the poem in this book in her magazine *Floating Bear*. The last address di Prima had for Martinelli was in Pacifica, California, in the seventies.

Joanna McClure (1930 –) was born Joanna Kinnison and grew up on her parents' U Circle desert ranch in the foothills of the Catalina Mountains near Oracle, Arizona. Her father lost the ranch during the Depression and moved to Tucson. She met Michael McClure when they were both students at the University of Arizona. After she divorced her first husband, Albert Hall, she moved to San Francisco and married McClure. She wrote her first poem in 1958. Her books—*Wolf Eyes* (Bearthm Press, 1974), *Extended Love Poem* (Arif Press, 1978), *Hard Edge* (Coffee House, 1987)—contain only a portion of her written work from 1960 on.

Barbara Moraff (1940 –) escaped an abusive family situation by surviving a horrible car wreck at age sixteen that nearly took her life but in the end empowered her. She suffered five years of plastic surgery to reconstruct her face. It was during this time that she read her work on the New York coffee-house circuit and published in *The Nation*, *Trobar*, *Femora*, *Origin*, and *Fuck You*. (She sometimes published as Barbara Ellen.) In 1961 Moraff moved to Vermont with her lover; together they built a small cabin. She appeared in *Four Young Lady Poets* (Totem/Corinth Press) the following year. She had a son in 1971 and stopped writing when he was diagnosed with cystic fibrosis, but eventually resumed writing poetry in 1976. She has worked as a potter, written a cookbook, taught meditation, and is an organic gardener. Her books include *The Life*, *Learning to Move*, *Telephone Company Repairman Poems*, *Deadly Nightshade* (Coffee House, 1988), *AHH* (Shadowplay, 1992), and *Potterwoman: Book Two*, *You've Got Me* (Longhouse, 1992). Her journal excerpts are included in *Ariadne's Thread* (Harper & Row, 1983). Now disabled and living on SSI in Danville, Vermont, Moraff is writing a pair of highly unusual books—a metaphysical mystery set in three different centuries and a ghost story about the house where she currently resides.

Brigid Murnaghan (? –) was born in the Bronx. She moved to MacDougal Street in Greenwich Village in 1948 and by 1984 had moved one block to Bleecker Street. She was the first film critic for the *Village Voice*. She runs a weekly salon in the Back Fence bar and hosts a Sunday poetry reading series. Her work appeared in Tuli Kupferberg's *Yeah* magazine, Seymour Krim's *The Beats*, and *Swank*. Brigid just completed "Paris & Baudelaire," a long poem, and has two novels in the works. She has two grown children.

Margaret Randall (1936 –) was born on December 6th in New York City. Her family moved to Albuquerque, New Mexico, when she was in sixth grade and she attended the University of New Mexico. She lived on the Lower East Side from 1958–61. A prolific writer, her books include *Giant of Tears* (1959), *Ecstasy is a Number* (1960), *Small Sounds From the Bass Fiddle* (1964), *Songs of the Grass*,

October, Water I Slip Into At Night, 25 stages of my spine (Elizabeth Press, 1967), *So Many Rooms Has a House* (New Rivers, 1968), *Part of the Solution* (New Directions, 1973), *Cuban Women Now* (The Women's Press, 1974), *We* (Smyrna Press, 1978), *Albuquerque: Coming Back to the USA* (Left Bank, 1986), *This is About Incest* (Firebrand, 1987), *Coming Home: Peace Without Complacency* (West End, 1990), *Walking to the Edge: Essays of Resistance* (South End, 1991), *Sandino's Daughter Revisited: Feminism in Nicaragua* (Rutgers, 1994). Between 1951 and 1985 she lived in Mexico City, Cuba, and Nicaragua. In 1989 she won a lengthy battle with the U.S. Immigration and Naturalization Service after it tried to deport her because of opinions expressed in her work.

Leo Skir (1932 –) was born Leo Joshua Skir on May 10th in Brooklyn, New York. He wrote for the early gay homophile press: *One, Tangents,* the New York *Mattachine Review,* and the *Ladder,* plus the straight press: *Commentary,* the *Evergreen Review, Mademoiselle.* He lived in Canada for a year (1973–75) researching the life of Esther Brandeau, the first Jew in Canada. Novels: *Boychick, Leo the Last, The Hours* (under the name of Lon Albert). He's lived in Minneapolis since '75 writing for the homophile press: *Gaze,* the *GLC Voice, Lavender Lifestyles, Equal Time, Focus Point.* Current projects: the novel *Esther Brandeau,* an anthology of Elise Cowen's poetry and the writings of her friends about her, a novel about the fifties, *Leo the Zionist,* plus an anthology of writings from the Stonewall Riots: *We're Freaking on In!*

Laura Ulewicz (1930 –) by nature a Bohemian, was born in Detroit into a Polish-American family. After experimenting with Chicago and New York, she settled in 1951 in San Francisco where she lived in the Haight and Golden Gate Park; worked as a camera girl in nightclubs and strip joints a few blocks from the soon-to-exist City Lights; hung out in North Beach; thought she was in heaven till the scene was publicized as "the Beat Generation" and the streets became full of pushy men eager for Free Love. Studied with Stanley Kunitz in Seattle, then landed in London where she met with THE GROUP at Lucie-Smith's and won a Guinness Poetry Award (money and publication of "The Inheritance"). She returned to the Haight in 1964 and worked at, then managed, then owned the I-Thou Coffee House and later the Root of Scarcity Herb-Grain-Coffee Store. She organized readings, art shows, etc., and had a radio program on KQED-FM interviewing writers. Settled in 1973 in the Sacramento Delta where she lives "fairly successfully in the Bronze Age" raising various kinds of garlic and everlasting flowers for sale at Farmers' Markets.

Janine Pommy Vega (1942 –) was born Janine Pommy on February 5th in Jersey City, New Jersey, to parents of Polish and Prussian extraction. Bored with high school, and having read Kerouac's *On the Road,* she came to New York City for weekends and hung out at the Cedar Bar where she met Gregory Corso. In February 1960 Janine graduated valedictorian of her high school class and then immediately took a bus to New York City. She shared an apartment for a time with Elise Cowen. She met the Peruvian painter Fernando Vega in 1962, they married in Israel, and lived in Paris and on the island of Ibiza until Fernando died of a heroin overdose in 1965. Her books include *Poems to Fernando* (City Lights, 1968), *Journal of a Hermit* (Cherry Valley Editions, 1979), *Morning Passage* (Telephone Books, 1976), *The Bard Owl* (Kulchur Foundation, 1980) and a new book forthcoming from City Lights, *Tracking the Serpent: A Pilgrimage to Four Continents*. She lives these days just outside Bearsville, New York.

Anne Waldman (1945 –) was born on April 2nd in Millville, New Jersey. Her father taught journalism at Pace College and her mother was active in the New York theater. Waldman grew up in Greenwich Village. She graduated from Bennington in 1966, moved into an apartment at St. Mark's Place on the Lower East Side, started the literary magazine *Angel Hair*, and later became director of the Poetry Project at St. Mark's Church in the Bowery. Her books include *Helping the Dreamer: New & Selected Poems 1966–1988* (Coffee House Press, 1989), *Baby Breakdown* (Bobbs-Merrill, 1970), *Giant Night* (Corinth Books, 1970), *Fast Speaking Woman* (City Lights, 1978), *Journals & Dreams: Poems* (Stonehill, 1976). Waldman recently edited *The Beat Book: Poems & Fiction from the Beat Generation* (Shambhala, 1996). Since 1974, she has been codirector with Allen Ginsberg of the Jack Kerouac School of Disembodied Poetics at the Naropa Institute in Boulder, Colorado.

ruth weiss (1928 –), a poet, performer, playwright, filmmaker, and painter, was born in Berlin and gave her first poetry with jazz reading in Chicago in 1949. She hitched to San Francisco in 1952 and has lived in the area ever since. In 1956 she innovated poetry with jazz at The Cellar. ruth still performs twice a week and won the Bay Area Poetry Slam in 1990. She wrote, directed, edited, and recorded a 16mm forty-minute black-and-white film *The Brink*, which was screened at the S.F. International Film Festival in 1961, at the Whitney Beat Culture exhibit in 1995, and the 1996 Venice Biennale Film Festival Retrospective Homage to the Beat generation. A frequent contributor to *Beatitude*, her work is also found in more than a hundred journals and magazines. Her books include *Steps* (Ellis Press, 1958), *Gallery of Women* (Adler Press, 1959), *South Pacific* (Adler Press, 1959), *Blue in Green* (Adler Press, 1960), *Light and other poems* (Peace & Pieces Press, 1976), *Desert Journal* (Good Gay Poets Press, 1977), and *Single Out* (D'Aurora Press, 1978). She has also written thirteen plays, of which six have been produced.

COPYRIGHT NOTICES

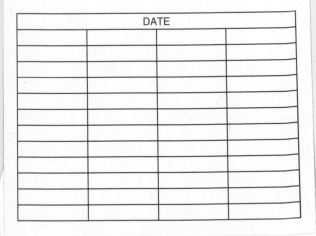